Her Russian Brute

Published by Rom Tell That

http://theodorataylor.com/

Copyright 2016 Theodora Taylor

ALL RIGHTS RESERVED

WARNING: The unauthorized reproduction or distribution of this copyrighted work is illegal. No part of this book may be used or reproduced electronically or in print without written permission, except in the case of brief quotations embodied in reviews.
This is a work of fiction. All names, characters, and places are fictitious. Any resemblance to actual events, locales, organizations, or persons, living or dead, is entirely coincidental.

Chapter 1

Ivan Rustanov was the current heavyweight extreme fighting (EFC) champion of the world. Nearly everyone who followed mixed martial arts fighting loved him. However, that evening, it was safe to say his family hated him.

Maybe it was because he'd completely forgotten the opera opening he was supposed to attend with them. Maybe it was because he didn't make it to their box until a full thirty minutes after the start of the performance (and that was only because he'd used his family name and his bodyguards to bend the opera house rules about latecomers not being allowed into the main theater). Or maybe it was because his "date" chose to wear a tight red dress that barely covered her ass.

Personally, Ivan appreciated the effort it must have taken Svetlana to not only walk without stumbling in her mile-high stilettos, but to also take her seat in the box without revealing her very naked crotch to the world. He'd

Her Russian Brute

told her not to wear panties when he texted her less than an hour ago. And to her credit—and considering her time constraints—the Ukrainian lingerie model reported for duty with admirable attention to detail.

However his mother and sister weren't remotely impressed.

"You *cannot* be serious," his mother, Yelena, hissed at him from her seat when Svetlana excused herself to "freshen up."

"You know all too well he is, Mother," his little sister, Marina, answered before her older brother could respond.

"Why can you not find nice girl to spend time with?" his mother demanded in a lowered voice. "You should date one of your sister's university friends. Nice girls from good families. Not harlots."

"My friends are far too smart to get involved with Ivan," his sister insisted.

She wishes, Ivan thought with an inner smirk. If only his sister knew how many of her friends he'd already slept with. He'd made it into a sort of game, checking at least two of them off of his inner list whenever he visited Marina at school.

His sister might consider herself above dating a fighter like him, but the rest of her friends were like moths to a flame with the boy who burned the baddest in their small circle of Russian elites. Her friends might have thought twice about openly admitting to his sister how much they liked the Rustanov with the chiseled face and 12-0 record, but did they melt underneath him as soon as he got them alone in a dark corner? Oh, *da*, they did.

As he watched Marina eye the seat Svetlana had vacated with frank distaste, he almost felt sorry for her. She would probably do exactly as his parents expected. Settle down with her boyfriend, the son of a fellow Russian elite. Make perfect little Russian elite babies. Do everything it took to further gloss over the fact that until a decade or so ago, the Rustanovs had been a century-old crime family before switching gears to become a highly successful legitimate operation.

And this was why his parents clearly preferred their dutiful daughter to their incorrigible son. Ivan might have a perfect knockout record, but his sister was the perfect soldier. Primed and ready to marry her boyfriend of two years as soon as they finished university. Whereas Ivan had dropped out of business school a mere two years in to

Her Russian Brute

pursue a career on the international fighting circuit.

He'd interned with his cousin, Boris, the summer before his third year of university, and Boris—who was a former underground fighter turned businessman—ended up training him. Now just a few years later, Ivan held a perfect record, and thanks to his good looks and bad boy reputation, he'd landed several endorsement contracts. Adding millions to the billions he already stood to inherit as a scion of one of the richest families in Russia.

Ivan was now arguably the most famous Rustanov in the world, even more so than his cousin Alexei, the man who currently ran the family empire from his compound in Texas. But that didn't stop his immediate family from regarding Ivan with disdain that night, as if he'd invited a leper—as opposed to an up-and-coming lingerie model— to the opera his family helped finance.

"This is not the kind of woman you bring out with you in public," his father told him during the intermission as they stood side-by-side in the men's restroom.

Normally a public restroom wouldn't be considered a private enough spot for a father and son to have this sort of exchange, especially during intermission in a crowded theater. But in this case, two of the family bodyguards

4

stood outside the restroom's front doors, giving all the other men who were desperate to pee "fuck-off" faces, while Ivan and his father took their sweet time at the urinals.

"You should find a nice girl, someone your mother likes, for public and take a pet for private."

"Just like you," Ivan said, knowing exactly where this conversation was headed.

"Just like a *Rustanov*," his father answered. "*Rustanovs* do not bring girls like that to the opera."

"Why not? I heard rumors Cousin Boris actually married his pet for a short time."

"Boris is only half, and maybe not right in the head. I think Alexei tolerates him because others are afraid of him, and that quality is good for conference room negotiations. But you have same qualities as Boris, and you are a full-blood. Plus, Boris has been off in the States for almost whole spring and summer this year. Soon, I feel, the time will come for him to step down and for you to step up in the Moscow office. Soon our *full* line could once again take over the Russian side of our empire."

His father zipped up his pants. "But not if you continue participating in these silly fights of yours."

Her Russian Brute

Ivan hated the way his father spoke of the cousin who'd trained him, and he barely kept himself from openly rolling his eyes at his father's dismissal of Ivan's career choices. MMA fighting was a billion dollar industry, yet his father referred to the sport as if it were simply a bunch of hot-headed children tussling inside a ring.

"You must return to university," his father insisted as they washed their hands. "Finish your business studies like your cousins, Boris and Alexei, so they will respect you."

He sneered at his son in the typical Rustanov way. "You are becoming too old for those fights. And your mother does not like these girls you bring around."

Like Ivan gave one fuck what his mother liked. If it were up to Yelena Rustanov, he'd only date girls who sat around drinking tea all day and telling her how pretty she still looked in her tennis outfits.

Yet, family was family…

He stayed for the rest of the performance, and even managed not to doze off thanks to a very subtle over-the-pants hand job from Svetlana. But as soon as they headed toward the limo line, he started making the necessary moves to depart.

"Svetlana has promised to make an appearance at a club opening tonight, and I will escort her there," he told his family while they waited for their limo outside the theater. They were, as always, placed at the front of the opera's busy pick-up line, even though they hadn't been the first to arrive for the performance. Just one of the many perks of being among the theater's most generous donors.

"But what about the opening night party?" his mother demanded as he kissed her on her rouged cheeks. "We are hosting it at the house. You must come!"

"Perhaps I will stop by later," he replied. Meaning, "perhaps I will stop by never."

Marina barely tolerated his kiss when he bent down to touch his lips to her cool cheek.

"Why must you always be such a bastard?" she hissed in his ear. "Is her life not hard enough?"

He merely gave his sister a cool look. Their mother had grown up rich and pampered and had only become more so over the years, thanks to Alexei's solid investment strategy and his knack for collecting ailing corporations during the last few economic downturns. With this money, their father had given Yelena everything she had ever wanted, save his fidelity.

7

Her Russian Brute

Ivan doubted 99.9% of the world—which was also the number of people who possessed less money than his family did—would feel *sorry* for his mother.

"I will text you the address of the club we are heading to," he answered his sister. "Stop by later if you become sick of being a bore."

Before she could respond, one of the guards informed them the family car had arrived.

Forever the dutiful child, Marina glared at Ivan as she followed their parents into the back of the sleek stretch limo.

The glare was wasted on him, however. He only spared his sister the minutest of glances before heading back towards the lobby. To rejoin Svetlana, who'd promised two of her friends would meet them at the club…and would be more than willing to do whatever it took to keep their favorite fighter thoroughly entertained.

No, he wasn't thinking about his family at all. In fact, he was already lazily turning toward what would surely be a coke-filled night of debauchery. Which was why the blast, when it came, only caught half of his face. Which was why the bomb, planted by his father's enemy, didn't kill his victim's entire family as intended. Only

Ivan's father, Ivan's mother, and Ivan's sister.

Ivan, the media claimed afterwards, had been lucky—suffering terrible but not fatal injuries.

Little did they know that despite his continued existence, Ivan hadn't survived the blast. That night, the devil-may-care fighter was killed. And in his place rose a vicious slaughterer. A brutal assassin. One so bloodthirsty, that the man who ordered the bombing, his soldiers, and his sons, would all die cursing his name and wishing, as he himself often did afterwards, he'd been in that limo.

Chapter 2

"It's not you, it's me, Scott," Sola told the caller as she reversed her mentor's car out of the strip mall parking space. "I feel like we're in two different places in our lives. You'll be joining a new team next season, and I still don't know where I'm going to land once I've graduated from ValArts. We both have these huge lives in front of us, and frankly, I think we're much too different to make things work together. We've been drifting apart for a while now. I think it's time for us to break it off. But I'll always think fondly of you, and, um…thanks, I guess…"

She cut her eyes towards the Lexus's Bluetooth display screen. "C'mon, say something! I'm dying here."

"Well…there's a lot of good stuff to work with, but you really shouldn't start a break-up speech with 'it's not you, it's me.' That's *so* cliché," her best friend, Anitra, answered.

"Okay, okay, good feedback," Sola said, mentally filing her friend's comment away.

Thank God she'd met the soon-to-be doctor during

her first year at ValArts, when Anitra had mistaken her as the only other black student in their Directing 101 course. After an awkward explanation about her heritage— Guatemalan parents, one of whom had curly hair and much darker skin, likely due to an ancestor of African descent, Anitra had answered, "Well, we're the only women wearing glasses in this class. So…"

So…they'd ended up becoming best friends. And remained such, even after Anitra dropped out of ValArts to attend school in West Virginia on a scholarship for a BS/MD Accelerated Medical Rural Health Program.

But luckily for Sola, the future doctor still remembered everything they'd learned during their first year Theater Lab course about providing critique and giving good notes.

"Anything else?" Sola asked, as she negotiated the car Brian had left at J.J.'s bar a few days ago out of the parking lot and onto one of Valencia's busier streets.

According to Brian, only a few decades ago Valencia had been home to nothing but a few goat farms, several orange groves, and a young art school: the Valencia Institute of the Arts. But thanks to the sprawl from nearby Los Angeles, the formally small desert town was becoming busier and busier by the year, and ValArts had gone on to become one of the most prestigious universities in the nation for students of both visual and performing arts.

"You're making it seem like it's mostly you who has all the issues in the relationship," Anitra said in response to Sola's question. "I'm concerned he's not going to realize what a douchebag he's been to you after you're done breaking up with him."

So much for giving good, impartial notes. "Nitra..."

"I'm just saying you might want to come right out and tell him he doesn't deserve you, because he's a controlling asshole who doesn't know a good hairstyle when he's sees it."

Sola shook her head at the radio. Anitra was still way more bitter about the second of only two major fights she and Scott had ever had over the course of their relationship.

Albeit, the hair one had been pretty major. Scott had lost it when she'd shown up at his condo in Marina Del Rey with her hair cut short after a summer spent interning with Brian in New Mexico. The ensuing argument became so intense, Sola ended up leaving early and taking a bus

12

back to Valencia. She spent the entire ride texting with Anitra about how insane Scott had been, yelling at her like a lunatic. Anitra agreed his reaction had been way out of line, too.

And when she'd told her mentor, Brian, what happened when she returned home earlier than expected, he'd said, "I think I can understand what a young woman such as yourself might see in a football player. It's a common enough trope, though in this case the handsome soldier is bearing pigskin instead of a sword. However, I don't think that fellow is for you, Marisol. I doubt he'd know *Tosca* from *Don Giovanni* if you gave him a libretto to follow along. And I'm sure Eddie would agree with me on this if he were able."

That was Brian's way of saying she could do better than Scott, and that if his husband, Eddie, weren't suffering from a rare debilitating neurological disorder that manifested in various states of dementia and catatonia—with the rare "good day" thrown in every few weeks or so—he'd totally agree.

Sola, too, had started to have doubts about what had, up until then, been a more or less fairytale relationship between her and the boyishly handsome second-string

13

Her Russian Brute

running back for the L.A. Suns.

But then Scott had shown up at the auditions of the thesis play she'd been stage managing to get in more tech hours, and finish what should have been a six-year program in only five. Even though the play was a spoken drama, he'd auditioned for the role of Sola's boyfriend with a charmingly off-key version of The Fray's "Over My Head."

Every other girl in the theater had melted and looked at Sola like she'd be crazy not to take him back. And so she had.

After all, he really did seem genuinely sorry, and at that point, they'd been together for over a year. Ever since meeting on a commercial she'd PA'd the summer before. Not that long ago, she'd been shocked that a sandy-haired football player from Omaha would even pay a nanosecond of attention to a poor Guatemalan art student like herself.

But just a year and a half after he sang for her forgiveness, Sola regretted not listening to Anitra and Brian. Scott had become more and more controlling since they'd gotten back together. Often calling to check up on her at odd times, and sometimes showing up at her place out of the blue.

She couldn't so much as mention a male, even in the context of one of her plays or classes, without him accusing her of cheating. In fact, the last two times they'd had sex, it had been because he'd shown up in the middle of the night without warning. Supposedly it was because he missed her. But Valencia was over an hour from where Scott lived in Marina Del Rey. And she could tell by the way he'd looked around the small cottage she rented for next to nothing from Brian, that he was searching for evidence that she'd been with another guy.

But the most damning fact of their doomed relationship was that Scott hadn't been able to spend any time with her since September. He was having a bad season with the Suns, and he'd told her not to visit him during the season because he "didn't want to be distracted by sex." Sola had been somewhat relieved, too, because with only a year left to complete the rest of her MFA requirements—including all her tech hours, since she'd have a thesis opera to direct during her spring semester— she'd be pretty busy herself.

However, being busy was one thing. Not missing your boyfriend one iota in over three sexless months was another. Which was why, as much as she hated to hurt

15

Her Russian Brute

anyone's feelings, she really needed to break up with him this weekend—the first one in thirteen they'd managed to schedule together.

But that didn't mean she wanted to stomp all over the guy.

"I just want to break up with him," she told her best friend as she carefully drove the short distance back to her little guesthouse, which sat just behind the Craftsman Brian shared with Eddie.

"I don't want to make him feel bad about himself. He's already upset about getting traded to Omaha after missing that pass in the playoff game. If I start listing reasons and stuff, it's going to be like I'm piling up on him."

"I guess," grumbled Anitra. "But I really think somebody ought to let him know that the shit he pulls with you isn't cool. Maybe I'll text him..."

"Anitra, don't you dare!" Sola insisted, knowing her bestie just might.

"Okay, okay, but only if you promise to call me right after. And take plenty of dialogue notes, because I want a blow-by-blow detail of what he says when you finally dump his sorry ass. That pixie cut was *so* cute!"

16

"Nitra…" Sola started to say with another laugh as she pulled up in front of the house.

But the laughter died in her throat when she saw what was waiting for her on the front lawn.

Scott, in all his gorgeous football player glory, stood there with what looked like at least half a marching band behind him. He smiled and the band started playing "Over My Head" as soon as her car came to a stop.

And just in case that wasn't enough of a clue about what was going on, two majorettes rolled out a sign that read, "MARRY ME, MARISOL!"

Sola's mouth dropped open.

And somewhere in the distance her best friend demanded on the other side of the car's Bluetooth radio,

"What's happening? What's going on?!"

Chapter 3

There is no one else to kill. Now you will have to decide how to live your life.

Ivan stood on the hill overlooking Wolfson Point, the small Idaho mountain town he now called home. Pondering, not for the first time, the last thing his older cousin, Boris, had written him. The two-line email had arrived shortly after he'd sent a one-line response to Boris's wife's heartfelt invitation to join the family in San Francisco for the holidays.

"No," he'd answered. Only to receive a rather ominous, and much less friendly, email from Boris a few minutes later.

He would have liked to dismiss his cousin's words. The musings of a formerly great fighter who'd slipped too easily into family life—just like his older half-brother, Alexei. But weeks later, standing behind the house he'd won in a card game earlier that year, Boris's words continued to haunt him.

There is no one else to kill.

After the murder of his family, Ivan had spent every waking moment either plotting to kill or killing. With Boris's help, Ivan had taken out the mafia boss who'd ordered the hit on his family, his entire small-time organization, and his three adult sons.

All that was left of that crime family now were the women and children. And Rustanovs didn't harm women and children.

Ivan wished there were still more men to kill. His fists reflexively opened and closed as he looked over the bucolic mountain town. Even now Ivan's hands longed to beat another person to death.

He'd become known for that. Beating the men who'd help bring about the death of his family into a bloody pulp before finally releasing them into the afterlife with two shots in the chest courtesy of his father's old GSh-18. Ivan's new take on the method the Rustanovs had become infamous for back when they'd still been a crime family.

Even Boris had been impressed with his young cousin's technique.

But not any more. Now Boris sent him terse emails that made Ivan feel like a petulant child for not accepting

the invitation to Christmas dinner. For refusing to pretend
he wasn't a monster. Something to be hidden away in the
dark—or in a dark house in the mountains of Idaho. One
did not invite monsters to Christmas dinner. Why couldn't
his cousin and his opera singer wife understand that?

"Sir, Hannah has a request."

Ivan looked over his shoulder. Gregory, one of the
servants who'd come with the house, stood behind him in
his usual ensemble of tailored pants and a cable knit
sweater worn over a tie and button down shirt. Yet in spite
of his relatively light attire, Gregory didn't show any signs
of feeling the biting chill of a winter day in Idaho, Ivan
noted. Not so much as a shiver, even though the freezing
wind was strong enough to blow the older man's formerly
lacquered gray hair into complete disarray.

"Yes, what is it?" Ivan asked, not bothering to keep
the irritation at being disturbed from his voice.

"Hannah would like to feed the prisoner, if you don't
mind, sir. She fears he might meet an untimely end before
he is able to stand before the judge."

The request, as with all of Gregory's requests, was
carefully worded. As if he were addressing a king rather
than some random guy who'd won this house and its

20

extensive property in a high-stakes poker game from Gregory's last boss. And Ivan had the feeling, not for the first time, that Thomas Wolfson—the man he'd won the manor from—wasn't just some unlucky sap who'd played his last desperate hand completely wrong. Mistaking Ivan's stony, Russian demeanor for bluffing, and going all in with the deed to his mountain manor house to cover his bets.

Back in Vegas, Wolfson had seemed like nothing more than a foolish man-child when he'd lost to Ivan. Even going so far as to cry and beg the Russian who'd just taken his house in a card game for the chance to win it back. The house had been with his family for generations, he'd tearfully told Ivan. Since the early 1800s. The whole town would be devastated when they found out a non-Wolfson now owned it. He had to let him win the house back. Or buy it back. He could raise the money, he'd insisted. Just give him a few weeks.

Ivan wasn't all that moved by his tears. Or the sight of a grown man, down on his knees, begging. For some reason, losing your whole family in a car bomb hardened your heart against men who didn't think before using their family's centuries-old home as collateral during a high-

Her Russian Brute

stakes card game.

Truth be told, the situation also hit a little too close to home. As Ivan discovered after the death of his family, his father had been concealing the real reason he was so desperate for Ivan to join the Rustanov family business. All those opera donations, the house in the north of Nevsky, the constant stream of beautiful women—pets—traded out before their thirtieth birthdays, the respect that came with being a member of one of the richest families in Russia…their father had gone deep into hock with the wrong people in order to keep up appearances.

The issue, as it turned out, was generational. Ivan's grandfather had been brought up as a crime family accountant. Ivan's father had assumed that he, like his father and his father before him, would be responsible for keeping the Rustanov money laundered and off the books.

But his father had been wrong in that assumption. When his nephew, Alexei, took over, he decided the only people who could touch the Rustanov fortune would be those with actual degrees and experience in investing. Of course, Alexei gave shares in the new company he'd created with the Rustanov holdings to everyone in the extended family. Shares that eventually made most of the family members billionaires, depending on when they sold them.

His father, as it turned out, had sold his shares embarrassingly early. And for millions as opposed to billions. But rather than go to his nephew for a loan when the millions ran out, he'd gone to an "old friend of the family." A friend who had been happy to extend Ivan's father several high-interest loans. Not everyone liked the Rustanovs sudden metamorphosis into a legitimate business family. And to this old friend, lending Ivan's father money had been like welcoming home a prodigal son. One who was more than willing to put his dusty laundering skills to secret use, against his nephew's express bidding.

But this old friend had been less than happy when he eventually discovered that not only was Ivan's father going through money too fast to ever pay him back in full, he'd also taken to skimming off the profits he laundered for the family.

So one of the skimmer's bodyguards had been bribed and outfitted with a bomb. A lesson served, and a warning to any other wayward Rustanovs who might think to take advantage of their old crime world connections.

Her Russian Brute

Big mistake.

That friend paid for his "lesson" with the lives of every single male member of his crime family over the age of 18. Now there was one less crime family to be taken advantage of, which when you think about it, probably wasn't the intention of that lesson at all.

It had taken Ivan nearly a year to avenge his family's deaths. Everyone who could possibly be punished for what happened was dead, but…

Ivan was still here.

With a murderous rage that still burned.

And no way to douse the flames.

So no, he hadn't given the spoiled rich kid his house back. In fact, Ivan moved in the very next weekend, and had been surprised to find it still fully furnished. His home in Nevsky had been outfitted in the same modern baroque style all the Rustanovs tended to favor. But this Idaho manor was a reflection of the country it resided in—one that had still been widely populated by indigenous nomads during the actual Baroque period.

The manor, though grand and sprawling across thirty-six acres of prime mountain real estate, was the kind of place built by people only a couple of generations away from doing everything with their hands. Exposed stone and wood for days, and not a hint of damask to be found on the walls.

Save for the gym, solarium, and Olympic-sized pool, it could not have been more opposite from his childhood home in Nevsky. Yet Ivan found himself settling into this new digs just fine. It was the perfect place for a recluse. It even came with two servants who lived in one of the property's detached cottages. When he'd come through the front door with Wolfson's deed in hand, they'd merely exchanged a look, then asked if he'd be in need of their services.

The two older servants had shown no signs whatsoever of missing the man Ivan replaced. In fact, they had been nothing but respectful and deferential during his months in residence. Even going so far as to turn away a few of the townspeople. The ones who came to the door yelling about how it wasn't right to have "one of his kind in the kingdom house."

Well, that is, the two servants had been nothing but deferential until now.

Ivan's eyes flickered toward the manor's strange outbuilding. It looked like a simple stone structure from the outside, but Ivan had been surprised during his original inspection of the property to find what appeared to be several jail cells inside, with just enough floor space left to create a narrow walkway in the middle. At first he assumed it was the site of the town's former jail, maybe a holdover from the 1800s. But inside the cells were cushioned floors and what looked a lot like oversized, silk-lined pet beds.

Yes, it was strange. But it had been the perfect place to throw the man he'd caught snooping around the property two days ago. A spy sent by his cousin, Alexei, to "check on him."

The man, overly thin, had been asked by his interfering cousin to get in and get out, and then provide a detailed report. Ivan could easily see why his cousin had sent this particular fellow to do the job.

The usual hire for the job would definitely have stood out in the small Idaho mountain town, but this short, spindly fellow with his sweater and jeans worn under a goose down parka, fit right in. If not for having made the bad decision to get very drunk at the town's only bar before completing his reconnaissance mission, his cousin's spy might very well have finished the job without detection.

However, Gregory noticed him staggering around the property almost as soon as he stepped foot on it and soon after that, Ivan had the whole story from him before tossing him in one of the cells.

But now it would seem Gregory's wife, Hannah, was having a fit of conscience.

"How many calories does someone need to survive?" Ivan asked.

"Fifteen to eighteen hundred, I believe, sir."

"Tell Hannah to give him fifteen hundred."

"Very well, sir." Gregory backed away with a small bow.

And Ivan, one side of his face numb with cold, the other numb for different reasons, went back to staring at the town below. With Cousin Boris's words still ringing in his ears: *There is no one else to kill. Now you will have to decide how to live your life.*

How did one even go about doing that when everything and everyone has been taken from you? When your past felt like someone else's life, and you couldn't see anything in your coming future but pain and regret? He didn't have a clue.

Her Russian Brute

Ivan glanced once more at the outbuilding. Wishing he could kill the prisoner inside. Use the man to temporarily relieve his constantly burning rage—at least for a little while. But that would only give Alexei the perfect excuse to come here in person, and a visit from his interfering, overly-concerned cousin was the last thing Ivan needed.

Boris and I are worried about you, he'd told Ivan after somehow finding the unlisted number for the house's only landline. *We thought you would recover after you had your revenge, but it is clear this has not happened.*

Nyet, he wasn't any better than he'd been during those months he'd spent waiting to recover from his wounds before he could take action. When he'd done little more than drink vodka and plot how he'd avenge his family's deaths once the burns on his face had healed. But now here he was, over two years later. He'd avenged the hell out of the murders of his parents and sister, but he felt more dead now. Now.....

There is no one else to kill. Now you will have to decide how to live your life.

He'd have Gregory release the man and drive him back down the mountain tomorrow, Ivan decided with a

28

huff of ice-cold air. A couple of hours before the only drivable road into town officially closed for the winter. It wouldn't open again until spring, which meant his cousin wouldn't be able to send anyone else to spy on him after Ivan returned the current fellow, weakened and the worse for wear after three days in an unheated jail cell.

It was a good plan. A decent, small revenge. But still…

Boris's words continued to burn in Ivan's head as he stood in the frigid cold, looking down on the town that didn't want him here.

Chapter 4

The world was on fire and someone was knocking to tell her to get out of the building. But the drums were banging too loud for Sola to find her way to the door.

Sola's eyes cracked open, only to immediately squeeze shut when confronted with the bright sun streaming in through her front room's window. This small action of squeezing her eyes shut hurt. As did raising a hand to her pounding head. Everything hurt. Everything was sore.

She tried again, slowly cracking her eyes open this time. Giving herself a few moments to adjust to the light. It only helped a little. She wasn't really in a burning building, but laid out under a sizzling patch of sunlight in her living room. That only brought on more questions. Why was she on the floor? How had she gotten there?

Had she been sleep walking again? *No*...she always returned to her bed after a sleep-walking episode. In fact, one of the major signs she'd been sleep walking was waking up in bed with her glasses on, an action so automatic, she literally did it in her sleep.

But she was on the living room floor, and the world was blurry. So she hadn't been sleep walking. What then?

The answers to all her questions came to her in sudden flash of shocking memories: Her shouting over the marching band to ask Scott if they could talk…how angry the clean-cut football player became when she tried to gently tell him she thought they should not get married, as he'd proposed, but instead break up.

"Do you know how lucky you are to have a guy like me asking you to marry him? Don't you get that?"

He'd kept saying this to her over and over, and at one point she'd had to point out, Anitra-style, that if she were really that lucky, he wouldn't have to keep reminding her how lucky she was.

That was when the weird accusations started flying. That she'd tricked him. That she was "talking back" to him. Followed up by the even more bizarre reassurances that everything would be okay, all of their problems would be solved, once she finished growing out her hair…and moved to Omaha with him in January.

Wait—what?!?! This had been the first Sola ever heard of this plan, and at that point she'd had to make it

Her Russian Brute

perfectly clear to Scott that she'd never, ever move to a place with zero opportunities to pursue her dreams of becoming an opera director.

His response? A small, nervous chuckle and, "That's not how I expected you to respond to my proposal, Sola. This is very disappointing. Very disappointing."

"I know, Scott. I am sorry. I'm really sorry, but I just think—"

That was when he punched her. Once. Twice. Three times. Each right hook had felt like getting hit with a mallet. Of course she'd fallen to the ground, only to have him start kicking her. That was the last thing she remembered. She must have blacked out.

And now she hurt everywhere. And someone was knocking at the door.

"Sola? Sola are you in there?" It was Vanessa, the kindly home aide who took care of Brian's husband while he was at work or out of town. She sounded worried.

Sola's eyes cut to her watch. But it was a weekend. Vanessa didn't work on weekends. In fact, Brian had purposefully scheduled this last business trip so he'd be back by Friday.

She forced herself to her hands and knees and was

32

happy to discover she could still stand. That meant Scott probably hadn't broken anything. Which she supposed was something to be thankful for, even if getting to her feet was still a blurry, bitch of a job.

Where were her glasses? she wondered as she took the first steps toward the door—only to hear an unwelcome crunching noise beneath the boots Eddie bought for her two Christmases ago. *Oh no!*

But no time to mourn their loss. She had to answer the door...

"Are you okay?" Vanessa demanded, her forehead furrowing with deep concern, when Sola opened the door.

"I'm fine. Long story," she answered, not quite knowing what else to say. Or how to explain this.

Should she call the police and file charges against Scott?

She dismissed the notion immediately. People who weren't exactly legally sanctioned to live in the United States didn't go to the police to file charges against men who were.

"Do you need a doctor?"

Vanessa's question brought Sola back out of her troubled thoughts.

Her Russian Brute

"No..." she forced herself to look like she wasn't in a crap-load of pain and asked Vanessa, "What's up? Is everything okay at the house?"

Brian's husband, Eddie, once a vibrant and energetic character actor turned college acting teacher, had been diagnosed with an extremely rare and completely debilitating disease a few years ago. To Sola, the orphaned student attending ValArts thanks to the California Dream Act, it had felt like she was losing yet another parent. Brian had been encouraging towards her from the beginning. In fact, he'd been the one to guide Sola, one of the few female Directing majors in his Musical Theatre Direction class, toward opera as a main interest for her future studies. And Eddie had taken it even further, not only drawing her into their formerly two-person fold, but also offering up their guesthouse to the undocumented student Brian had decided to take under his wing.

Eddie had attended every single performance Sola directed up until he'd been confined to a wheelchair. And on his better days, he'd still pepper Sola with questions about her latest projects and insist he'd make it to the next show, often just minutes before sinking back into a catatonic state.

34

For these reasons and more, Sola felt like a daughter to Brian and Eddie. Which was why she was much more concerned about Eddie than her own bruised and mottled face as she peered down at the petite home aide.

"Oh no, please no worry, Sola. Mr. Eddie is fine," Vanessa assured her in deeply accented English. Then she switched to Spanish to ask, "But do you know where Senor Brian is?"

"He did not come home last night?" Sola asked, switching to Spanish as well, although hers, unlike Vanessa's, was spoken with a strong Guatemalan accent.

Brian had gone on a business trip—something about an Idaho scout job for Alexei Rustanov, the billionaire who'd financed the new work Brian had directed at the Santa Fe Opera the summer before last. But he was supposed to have returned yesterday evening.

In fact, Sola had arranged for a shuttle to pick him up from the Van Nuys airport since she was supposed to be driving down to Marina Del Rey that evening break up with Scott. But Scott had shown up here with his marching band proposal, and apparently, Brian hadn't gotten on the shuttle…

So twelve plus hours after Brian was due back, Sola

Her Russian Brute

put on a pair of old, faded tortoiseshell glasses from about two prescriptions ago, and tried to locate him using the Find My Friends app she'd made him download after a few too many missed rehearsal calls in New Mexico. But it only said his phone couldn't be located.

Sola's stomach rolled with the image of Brian drunk in some Idaho bar. She knew it had been a bad idea to let him go there by himself. Brian had been super vague about the assignment, and she suspected that Alexei trusted Brian more than he perhaps should or would have if he'd known just how much covering Sola had done for him that summer in New Mexico.

But she'd had one last final to take on the Thursday he'd left, and her Math for Artists professor hadn't been feeling all that magnanimous. He'd told her in no uncertain terms that no, she couldn't reschedule the final for a class she'd put off until the second-to-last semester of the school year in order to accompany another professor on his business trip to Idaho, of all places. And with Eddie's medical bills piling up, Brian had definitely needed the extra money, so Sola had let him go alone.

But she was deeply regretting that decision now. After making a few calls, Sola discovered Brian had picked up his rental car once he'd arrived in Idaho but there was no trace of where he'd gone after that. The rental agency said they weren't allowed to disclose customer information. And the Idaho police department hadn't been any more helpful.

Her mistake had been in telling them her missing person wasn't a hiker. Because unless he was a hiker, a person needed to be missing for at least seventy-two hours before the police would start a formal search, and Brian had only been gone for forty-eight.

That was how she found herself on the mainframe in Brian's extremely cluttered home office a short while later. Sweeping empty bottles of bourbon off his desk and hoping to God he was one of those people who'd opted to let his browser save his passwords.

He wasn't. *Dammit*! But a few minutes of frantic searching later, Sola found a small index card with all his passwords written down in precise, legible handwriting. Yes! Old people were the best!

She typed in the user name and password for his online credit card account and went through his most recent charges. No hotel, she noted, but there was a charge from a bar called The Thirsty Wolf...a rather large charge.

Her Russian Brute

Of course there was. Sola had picked Brian up from enough New Mexico and Valencia bar floors to know how deliriously drunk he could get when he wasn't caring for Eddie. Visions of him on a random bar floor, being stepped over by strangers, assaulted her already pounding head as she looked up the bar's phone number. She punched the numbers into her cell phone, and waited for someone to pick up.

"Thirsty Wolf, how can I help you?"

"Hello, do you have a customer there by the name of Brian Krantz? I'm his—his daughter," she lied, just to make the conversation go more smoothly "I'm concerned about him because the last charge on his card was at this bar and he hasn't returned home yet."

"Oh hell," said the leathery male voice on the other end of the line. She heard the raspy sound of what she could only assume was a hand being placed over the receiver, and then the same voice, now muffled, yelling, "Ma! That outsider the Russkie's got holed up at the kingdom house has a daughter. And she's on the line, wanting to know where he is!"

"Well, don't just announce all our business to everyone," came another muffled, more distant, voice.

38

"Here, give me that phone!"

There was the brief sound of muttering and the phone being handed off, then: "Hello, this is Lorraine," a woman said, her voice equally as leathery as the previous man's but with a slightly more feminine lilt to it. "How can I help you?"

Sola looked down at the phone in her hand, truly alarmed. "Did I just hear you say Bri- I mean, my father, is being held by a Russian at some house in your town?"

"Yeah, sweetie, I'm afraid you did," Lorraine answered with a loud tsk that spoke volumes to Sola.

"Is it against his will?" Sola felt compelled to ask, since it had been a Russian who'd sent Brian on this job in the first place.

"I'm pretty sure he doesn't want to be there if that's what you're asking," Lorraine answered dryly. "Let me tell you, honey…that Russkie Monster is a piece of work. He caught your poor father trespassing on his property and threw him right into a cage! Judge don't come back through town until the spring thaw, so I guess your dad's just going to have to stay where he is until March, at the earliest. That's when Old Farris will be able to hear his side of the story. But don't you worry, Old Farris doesn't

Her Russian Brute

want outsiders hanging around Wolfson Point any more than the rest of us do. He'll probably tell that crazy Russkie he's got to let your daddy go. I never did like them damn Russians. You ever seen *Rocky 4*?"

"No," Sola admitted, still trying to wrap her confused brain around what she'd just been told.

"Well you should, because then you'd see what I mean. They've got no business on American soil, taking over kingdom houses that don't belong to them, and pissing all over folks! I don't even understand how he's allowed to be here in the first place, let alone own property!"

As a person who still didn't have a clear path to United States citizenship after her upcoming graduation and who didn't look a thing like the man she claimed was her father, she carefully steered the conversation down a safer path.

"The thing is, we can't wait until March. His hus— uh, my mom—is very sick," Sola felt guilty about lying, but like Brian always said, "direct for your audience, not yourself." And the Russian-hating woman on the other side of the phone didn't exactly sound progressive. "He needs to take care of her. He also has classes he's

40

supposed to teach out here in California. Are you sure there's nothing that can be done?"

"I don't know. You cute?"

Sola blinked. "Um, what?"

"What I mean is, if you're cute, you could go up there. Pretend to be a hooker. Or something like that. Those are the only kind of women been up to the kingdom house since he moved in."

Hookers? Kingdom house? She was so confused.

"Listen," she told the odd woman on the other side of the line. "This Russian man cannot keep my father there against his will. That's called abduction. He has a partner and a job and people who love him. I am sure this is all just a big misunderstanding and I know I can help clear things up. Just hold on…I'm coming."

"Okay, well, come on out here if you want, sweetie," Lorraine said, not sounding very optimistic about the prospect of Sola being able to get Brian out of jail—or the Russkie's house, or wherever the hell he was being held. "But you better come quick. The only road into or out of town closes at 6:00 PM sharp tonight."

Chapter 5

"Wait, wait, wait! You're heading to a town in *Idaho* with only one road? And that one road will close tonight for the entire winter? Seriously?!" Anitra asked incredulously on the other side of the line. "And I thought West Virginia was backwards…"

"I know, right?" Sola replied into the small microphone attached to her earbuds. "And I've only got, like, a few hours to get Brian out of there or we'll both be stuck in that place until spring!"

"Wasn't there a movie kind of like that? What was it called…?"

"I have no idea, " Sola answered, nervously eyeing the increasingly mountainous scenery outside the shuttle windows. Any other day, she would have found the snow-capped mountains, so different from the retrofitted desert she called home, awe-inspiring and beautiful. But now, as the sun began to descend behind the jagged peaks, they just seemed ominous.

It had been a hard scramble to get to Idaho. First,

she'd had to find a non-stop flight to Boise. Then drive all the way to LAX to catch it. And apparently the debit card gods hadn't felt like she'd bled nearly enough money, because now she was trapped in an airport shuttle with a driver who kept asking her, "Wolfson Point? You sure that's where you want to go? You know the road out of there's closing in a few hours, right?"

Finally, in a last ditch attempt to get out of reassuring the driver yet again that yes, Wolfson Point was exactly where she wanted to go, she called her best friend. However, less than a minute into her conversation with Anitra, Sola's stomach began to knot up tightly with dread.

"*Seven Brides for Seven Brothers*!"

"What?"

"That's the name of the movie. It's about these seven brothers—six really, because the oldest is already married to some woman he met in town. Anyway, this dude and his six younger brothers—they're all like these wild mountain men who can sing and dance really well…cause, you know, *that* happens—come up with this plan to kidnap a bunch of women, and then they cause an avalanche over the mountain pass so they can keep the girls there until spring."

Her Russian Brute

"And what happens?" Sola asked, interested despite herself. "Do the women get rescued?"

"No! They end up staying there until spring. Then they marry the brothers." Anitra sucked on her teeth as if she were just now seriously thinking about the film's storyline for the first time ever. "Really, that movie should have been called *Stockholm Syndrome for Seven Sisters*."

Sola looked at her phone, wondering—not for the first time—whether she should consider finding a best friend who didn't live on the other side of the country, and perhaps more importantly, didn't tell her about movies featuring young women being successfully kidnapped by wild mountain men. "Anitra, why would you even tell me that story right now?"

"I'm just saying if you bump into this Russian guy and he's got six brothers—run."

Chapter 6

"You like that, Ivan? Like how I give good blowjob?"

"*Da*," Ivan answered, carelessly fisting the hair of the girl sucking his dick while his restless gaze scanned the room.

He soon spotted a tall, red-haired woman in a tight pink dress standing between the men and women's bathrooms. She was texting and looked bored. He'd change that.

Ivan deliberately stared at her until she finally looked up from her phone. Her mouth formed into a little 'o' when she realized whose eye she'd caught—and what was being done to him by another beautiful woman while he stared at her.

"Go faster," he commanded, guiding the head of the woman sucking him off. His eyes stayed on the redhead, he jerked the other girl's head up and down on his dick until he felt the familiar tingle at the base of his spine.

The fight or the fuck, as his cousin Boris said. Most

Her Russian Brute

nights, Ivan chose the fight. But nights like this were the best of all. Earlier that evening he'd sealed his position as the EFC's official heavyweight champion of the world. And now…

He pulled his cock out of the young woman's wet mouth… And now he was about to jizz all over one pretty blonde's face, while a redhead in a pink "fuck me" dress watched. A second later, the blonde's face was covered with his load. She smiled up at him, her long tongue sweeping sensually across her mouth. Painting the perfect dirty picture.

Too bad it was wasted on him. He was already zipping up his pants and heading over to where the redhead still stood, her mouth partly open.

"Come here," he said, roping one arm around her small waist and pulling her to him. He motioned to one of his guards, who being well trained, automatically handed him a small vial.

"Hello, baby," he said to the redhead with a grin. Then he dipped his head close into her neck, using her long, red extensions to cover the bump of cocaine he took from the vial. His next fight hadn't been scheduled yet and regardless, it would be a good six to eight months before

46

he had to undergo another drug test. Plus, his chances of getting hit with a random drug test before the cocaine left his system were almost nil. Between his fame and his family name, the EFC officials wouldn't dare.

Yet he wasn't surprised when his cousin Boris appeared soon after Ivan took the bump.

"You should be more careful with that substance," Boris told Ivan, looking around the nightclub with bored, hooded eyes. "Your soft EFC would ban you from fighting if they ever found out."

Boris was, as far as Ivan knew, a never-defeated old school underground fighter. As such, the EFC was far too glitzy for him. Give Boris a basement and an illegal betting ring, and he'd show you exactly why everyone called him The Russian Beast—inside the boardroom and out.

Ivan, however, liked the glitz and glamour that came with being a world-renowned pro-fighter. The glitz, the glamour, *and* the girls. Oh, how he liked the girls.

It showed how much he respected Boris that instead of spinning the redhead into the nearest wall to take her dress up on its invitation, he slapped her ass and told her to wait for him back in VIP.

47

Her Russian Brute

"You can rest your mind, Boris. I was careful," he said when she was gone. "No one saw."

"I saw, Ivan," he pointed out. "And in any case, it does not matter. You know they can test randomly at any time."

"I am in Russia. My homeland. No one would dare."

Boris could have argued this point, but they both knew Ivan was right. Instead, he said, "I am going now. It is late."

"It is not that late," Ivan countered. "And you are the one throwing this party for me. Do not be like Alexei. Stay! Fuck some girls!"

Boris only looked around the room as if it were filled with rotting fish and not scores of Russia's most beautiful woman. "I have early morning. I will see you on Monday for training."

Business, training, and fighting. That was all Boris ever cared about. What a bore his cousin was. Ivan wondered if he'd ever cut loose and had any fun. Maybe back in his twenties when he had that beautiful black pet the rest of the family disapproved of? *Probably not*, Ivan thought with a mocking sneer.

Truthfully, Ivan loved his cousin and respected the

48

hell out of him. But Boris wasn't good for much more than training and dark, brooding looks.

"Okay, go. Be boring," Ivan said with a grin. "I will fuck enough girls for both of us. And I will make sure to take care of some business, too…"

Then he cupped his hands around his mouth and yelled out: "Who wants to interview to become a Rustanov pet tonight?"

The room full of beautiful women erupted in a cheer. *Da*, he was back in his homeland after a grueling world tour. A place where every young Russian woman knew that becoming a Rustanov pet was the golden ticket to a life full of beautiful clothes, opulent travel, and whatever other luxuries she might imagine—including a few she couldn't.

Ivan headed over to his VIP lounge and had his dick buried in the redhead before his cousin was even out the door.

He turned to a huge mirror in the Moroccan-themed nightclub to watch as he fucked this latest girl. It was like staring at a piece of moving artwork. He was beautiful. She was beautiful. What could be more aesthetically pleasing than to watch them go at it together?

He smiled at his image in the huge mirror, only to recoil. A monster stared back at him.

"Sir?" it said. *"Sir, are you awake?"*

Ivan sat up in his bed with a sharp inhale. He immediately reached up to touch his face, only to have his heart sink when his hand found the scars. They never featured in the dreams of his old life—at least not until the dreams transformed into a nightmares.

One side of his face was still that of the beautiful heavyweight fighter everyone had cheered for. The other was…ugly, red, mottled flesh. *Da*, on the other side of the dream, Ivan was still the man he'd once heard a local refer to as, "The Russkie Monster."

More knocking. "Sir? It's Gregory. May I come in?"

A whispered expletive fell from Ivan's lips. What did the man want?

"I asked not to be disturbed."

"I know, sir, but it's getting rather late. The access road will be closing soon, and…" He hesitated before saying the next thing, as if he was finding it hard to believe himself. "And…I believe there's another human—I mean another *person*—on the property. And sir…I'm, ah…sensing it's a female…"

50

Chapter 7

What the freaking heck? Sola wondered as she crept into the outbuilding.

She'd thought of going straight up to the front door after the driver dropped her off at The Thirsty Wolf. But a quick chat with Lorraine at The Thirsty Wolf quickly changed her mind.

"Rumor is the Russkie's keeping your daddy in the outbuilding behind the big house. If it was me looking for my kin, I'd go straight there instead of trying to deal directly with that bastard and his turncoat servants."

Technically, Lorraine was an older woman in her 50s or 60s. But she had a craggy, wind-worn face and a strong edge to her that let Sola and probably anyone else who came into this establishment know she wasn't someone to be messed with. And though Sola didn't actually see a shotgun, she could sense one lurking just behind the scratched up bar.

The bar itself, though small and dark, had a certain vintage charm. A simple wood framed mirror took up most

Her Russian Brute

of the back wall, and was surrounded by a cluster of old seventies wolf paintings with several pairs of what looked like handmade snowshoes thrown into the mix.

Eclectic, to say the least. The kind of place the hipsters at ValArts would love, even though this place wasn't trying to be ironic with its décor. There was a handwritten chalkboard menu in the midst of the wall decor. Supposedly they were offering lamb stew as the main course tonight. But no one had taken Sola's order. Or even offered so much as a drink since she walked in and gingerly sat down on one of the rough, carved oak barstools.

Instead, Sola felt the eyes of every patron on her back, and the bar became silent as a stone until Lorraine came over to speak with her.

"Have you tried going up there on your own yet?" Lorraine had asked with a frown.

"Nope, she just got here," answered one of the bar patrons behind her.

Sola glanced over her shoulder to see a man in a short-sleeved plaid button up. He nodded toward the bar's single front window. "Saw her get off the shuttle myself."

"Well, at least we don't have to add assault to the

Russkie's list of offenses, I guess," Lorraine grumbled. Though she didn't sound at all as pleased about this as Sola imagined she would.

Meanwhile, everyone in the bar continued to stare at them. No, not at them. *Her*. Just Sola. And Sola couldn't help but think of every horror movie she'd ever seen set in small remote town, just like this one.

Suppressing a shiver, she told Lorraine, "Um, I just need directions to where my father is being kept. Then hopefully we can get out of here."

"I can give you directions," Lorraine answered, "But if you're serious about rescuing your dad, your best bet is to break him out of that cage. Don't bother going up to the big house. Especially seeing as how the main road is scheduled to close in less than two hours from now."

"I already seen the sheriff headed down there," the man by the window called out helpfully.

Lorraine nodded. "So you have to hurry. And you definitely don't have time to argue with that Russkie bastard. Here, I've got just the thing for you…"

Lorraine bent down behind the bar and came back up with a skeleton key. It was old and slightly rusted with a two-pronged bit.

Her Russian Brute

"My grandpappy used to tend the stables up there back when the Wolfson family still kept horses for getting around town. This is a skeleton key and he told me it could open the lock of every building on that property."

Whoa, Sola had thought, taking the key. She was definitely not in California anymore. She couldn't even imagine a structure with locks so old that a skeleton key worked on them. With the eyes of all those people on her, Sola had decided to take Lorraine's advice, and now the key felt heavy as hell inside the pocket of her tweed jacket.

The trip up the smallish hill to the main house overlooking the town had been an effort and a half. She must have burned at least a few thousand calories trekking up the snow-covered road towards the huge manor and then around that to the collection of buildings in the back. There was an old barn, which she imagined housed the horses Lorraine had mentioned earlier. There was also a charming little cottage, and a few other structures. But she immediately sensed the small, dull red building with its iron door was the place she was looking for, and she headed toward it.

After unlocking it with the skeleton and then putting considerable effort into yanking the heavy door open, she

54

was confronted with a pitch-black interior and a deep cold unlike anything she'd ever known. Literally. She'd grown up in Guatemala and California, and she was fast discovering that her hoodie, tweed jacket, and faux raccoon hat ensemble wasn't nearly enough to handle the frigid air inside the building.

Shivering, she turned on her phone's flashlight, only to go even colder when she saw the row of floor-to-ceiling cells lining the back wall.

"Brian?" she called out softly, hoping like hell he wasn't anywhere near this cold, dank place. But no such luck.

"Sola?" a wobbly voice called out from the cell on the back wall, the farthest one from the door. "Is that you?"

She ran to the cell and found Brian huddled on the floor on top of what looked like a very large doggie bed. He was wrapped in a thick, wool blanket and dressed a lot more warmly than her in a flannel cap, gloves, a down parka, and hiking boots. But still…

"Brian, oh my God! Who did this to you?"

"Someone bad. Sola, you have to get out of here. Before he finds you. I don't know how you found me. In

Her Russian Brute

fact, I'm wondering if you're a hallucination, but just in case you aren't, dear girl, I beg of you…go. Go now!"

"What? No way! You actually think I'd leave you here? Look, I've got a key and you're coming with me!"

She tucked the phone under her chin and went to work, placing the skeleton key in the lock. It was hard going. Her hands shook with cold and she really had to shove in the key, putting her whole arm into turning the heavy lock.

But she managed in the end.

"C'mon," she said, flinging open the cell door and rushing in to help the older man to his feet.

"What happened to your face?" Brian demanded when he got a closer look at her.

"I'll tell you in the car. Your rental is parked at the bar. Do you still have the keys?"

"Yes, they're in my pocket. Thank goodness that brute didn't take them."

Yes, thank goodness, she thought, guiding him out of the cell and toward the main door. But she was well aware that whatever monster locked Brian in that cage was still lurking around on the property.

"We've still got some time before the road closes, if

56

we move fast we can—"

She'd turned to glance back at Brian who was slowly shuffling behind her. And walked right into a hard wall. So hard, her bruised face screamed in protest as she stumbled backwards, almost losing her footing completely.

"What the…?!"

She raised her phone flashlight to look up…then up some more.

A man stood there. So huge, she immediately knew who he was. And why Lorraine called him the Russkie Monster. He had to be six-foot-five—maybe even taller. He had long, crazy wolfman blond hair. It looked like it hadn't been combed in days. Maybe not ever. And he reeked of what smelled like a semi-permanent cologne made up of sweat and alcohol. Half his face was mottled and red, like it had been covered in Freddy Krueger make-up, but on closer examination, she could see it wasn't make-up. No, definitely not make-up.

So that was why they called him a monster. He stood there, looming over her, larger than life. And breathing fast and hard.

Like a beast awoken.

He raised some kind of old timey oil lamp, and Sola

Her Russian Brute

squinted against it's sudden light.

"Who are you?" the monster demanded, his voice little more than a dark snarl. "And what are you doing here?"

Chapter 8

She shined her ridiculously small phone light at him, and he shined his much larger one at her. What he saw caused his breath to catch.

A girl, *da*, just as Gregory had said, but her moon-shaped face was like his. Beautiful on one side, but destroyed on the other.

One side was lovely. With bronzed skin, a wide nose, and brown eyes so big, he could still see them clearly behind a pair of large tortoiseshell glasses, even in the shadows. But the other side of her face was destroyed. No, not destroyed, he realized after a moment, but heavily damaged. Covered in green and blue bruises and very swollen. He'd seen this kind of bruising before, too many times to count. He'd usually been the one inflicting it. But never on a woman.

Based on the girl's small and plump stature, along with her glasses, he doubted she was a fighter. No, somebody had punched her. More than once. With what looked like a solid hook.

Her Russian Brute

He stared at her in the light of his lamp, and she stared at him, both obviously taken aback by what they were seeing.

He opened his mouth to once again ask what she was doing here. Only to be caught off guard when she suddenly shoved him backwards.

"What the hell is wrong with you?!" she demanded. "Are you crazy or something? Huh? Caging Brian up like he's some kind of dog!?"

Ivan glared at her, and suddenly understood the American term, "spitfire."

"This man was on *my* property. Not only trespassing, but spying on me. This town has strict laws about trespassing. By all rights—"

"Are you freaking kidding me?! Nobody has the right to keep a person locked up in an unheated building without a real bed or access to food, water, and a toilet. Brian has asthma and he's over sixty years old!"

"No need to bring my age into this discussion," the prisoner, who Ivan could now see had probably dyed his graying hair brown, said behind her.

"Shut it, Brian!" she returned over her shoulder. "Now is not the time for vanity! The point is, he's a

60

monster for caging you up like this."

The girl turned back to Ivan, her eyes blazing with righteous indignation. "What kind of person does this to another human being?" she demanded.

"The kind of human being who finds a drunken *spy* on his property. And now I have *two* trespassers."

His voice was hard enough to convey threat, but inside, his mind was scrambling with questions. *Who was she? How did she know the prisoner? Why wasn't she flinching at his face?* He knew she could see it clearly by now.

But all she said in the wake of his implied threat was, "Look, you have to let him go. He's got a sick spouse at home. And classes to teach. People who love him."

A teacher. *Alexei had sent a teacher to spy on him?!?*

"Why would Alexei send a teacher to spy on me?" Ivan asked her, finding this latest bit of information nearly impossible to believe.

The girl stopped, clearly wondering the very same thing. They both looked at the older man and she said, "Brian…?"

A beat of silence, then the man said, "Well, I might

Her Russian Brute

have slightly exaggerated my contributions during the Vietnam War."

The young woman let out an exasperated groan. "Oh Brian, please tell me you didn't give Alexei-freaking-Rustanov that bogus spy story!"

"It's not bogus, dear girl. I delivered quite a few secret messages during that war!"

"Brian, you were a signalman—not a spy! And you delivered messages with *flags*! I can't believe you agreed to do this!"

"We didn't really use flags. I was in the Army, not the Navy—we had to erect our own *radio* towers, you know," Brian replied testily. "Ask anyone, dear girl. We signalmen were a most valuable part of the war effort in Vietnam—!"

"Okay, okay, Brian…just please stop talking," She shook her head and held up her hand at the older man before turning back to face Ivan. And to his surprise, she once again met his eyes with seemingly no trouble at all.

"So apparently he really *was* trespassing, but obviously you can see he's harmless…"

"Harmless! I am hardly harmless," the older man complained behind her. "If not for that ill-advised drink of

62

Dutch courage at that sad establishment that passes for a bar in this town, I most likely would have completed my mission—"

"The point is, you can't keep him here," the girl told Ivan, speaking over the offended man as if he were nothing more than a frustrated child.

She continued to hold Ivan's gaze, fighting for the old man despite his foolishness and despite the obviously painful injuries to her face, which confused Ivan even more. Who was this girl? And why wasn't she afraid of him?

But somehow he managed to keep his expression as aloof and detached as possible, determined not to let his confusion show. "If the judge tells me I should release this man, then I will," he informed her.

"When does the judge get here?"

"In the spring."

"Great, we'll come back then."

She grabbed the prisoner's arm and started to move forward, probably hoping to take Ivan by surprise again.

But not this time. He got in front of her before she could take so much as two steps.

"He is my prisoner, and you have no rights here. I

Her Russian Brute

was thinking of letting him go before you showed up. But you have pissed me off, so now he stays until spring."

Her eyes widened, "What? That is ridiculous, not to mention grossly unfair—"

But then she stopped. Ivan got the feeling she wasn't the kind of person who railed against life's unfairness by the way her eyes darted back and forth. He could almost see her mind working over what he'd just said, as if the situation were a math problem she was trying to solve.

"No, I can't leave him here," she mumbled, seemingly to herself. "Eddie is sick and he needs him." She shook her head as if making a final decision. "No, no, I can't leave him here…"

She looked up at Ivan and said, "So how about if I stay here in his place? Like as collateral."

Ivan blinked. Half sure he hadn't heard her correctly. "You are offering to stay here with me?" he asked, not quite believing his ears. "Until the judge comes in the spring?"

64

Chapter 9

At the same time, Brian cried out, "No, dear girl, you have school! You're almost done with your classes! And this is no place for you."

"Yes, I have school and you have Eddie," Sola responded. "One will still be there when I get home in the spring, but one might not."

"I can't let you do this. He's a monster. His servants have barely fed me enough to survive. I can't let them do the same to you."

"Brian," she said, taking her worried mentor by the arms. "You are like a father to me. You believed in me when no one else did. And I know you don't want to hear this, but I'm young and I'm strong and I don't have anybody waiting for me back in Valencia. You have Eddie and your students. I can easily survive a few months in this cell, but if anything happened to you…"

Her eyes teared up at the thought of any harm coming to the man who'd seen a director with promise where other professors had only seen a poor undocumented Guatemalan who'd somehow gotten into the most prestigious art school in California—perhaps only to fill some quota. She shook her head at him, insisting, "You have to let me do this. You have to go. You know you have to go, and we don't have time to argue about it."

"No, you do not," The Russian said, butting into to their conversation. He regarded them with hooded eyes and a bored sneer, like her and Brian's drama wasn't interesting enough for him.

"Also, I have not said whether I will accept the trade."

She threw him a murderous look. Let him try to keep Brian here even one more freaking moment. He might be the big, scary monster in this situation, but she'd lost everyone she loved by the age of fourteen. She knew how to fight for the few people in life who were precious to her. And Brian and Eddie were definitely precious to her.

Judge be damned. She'd punch this guy in the throat with Brian's car keys before she'd let him keep Brian here even a second longer.

She took a step forward, prepared to do just that.

But then the large Russian turned and yelled over his shoulder. "Gregory, are you still out there?"

"Yes, sir," came a voice just beyond the building's open door.

"Please escort my cousin's spy to his rental car. Miss..."

He looked down at her, waiting for her name.

"Sola," she answered, giving him her nickname, not to be friendly, but because the less this crazy dude knew about her, the better.

"Sola," he repeated with a familiar sneer. It reminded her of Alexei Rustanov, the Texas billionaire by way of Russia, who'd funded the opera she and Brian had worked on last summer.

Hang on…Alexei Rustanov was Russian, too. Were these two somehow related? And if so, why had Alexei sent Brian to spy on him?

"*Sola* will be staying here in our prisoner's stead until the judge comes in the spring. Escort Mr. Krantz out of town."

"Yes, right away, sir," the voice said, betraying no sign of surprise whatsoever.

"Go, Brian…" she said, pressing the keys into his hand before he could argue with her again. "We've only got an hour until the road closes, and Eddie is waiting for

Her Russian Brute

you. I'm not leaving. And if both of us disappear, Eddie won't have anyone."

Brian must have seen her point, because he finally started walking. "I'll be in contact with Alexei Rustanov. He got me into this, I'll make sure he gets you out of it."

She could only smile. He might be asthmatic and cold, but nothing—not even a crazy Russian—could keep signalman-turned-director Brian Krantz from delivering a dramatic line as he made his exit.

Still, she kept her eyes on the Russian as Brian moved past the hulking man to the outbuilding's door.

He'd agreed to her bargain, but seriously this dude was acting exactly like a villain in a bad action movie. And she'd sat through enough of those with Scott to know they were the kinds of guys who would pretend to agree, only to snap a hostage's neck when you tried to make the exchange.

And this guy could definitely snap poor Brian's neck. Even though he was wearing a pea coat, Sola could see those were muscles, not fat, underneath all that wool. Stretching the fabric so wide, she had to wonder if the coat, which fit perfectly, had been custom tailored for him. Being from California, she didn't know much about winter coats, but she highly doubted there were many high-quality coats available that fit that well for guys as big as him.

To his credit, the Russian let Brian slide past him with barely more than a small sneer. *It must be a family trait*, she thought, remembering every time she'd been sneered at by Alexei Rustanov, the domineering billionaire who expected everyone to do exactly as he said.

They stood like that in their wildly mismatched stand-off. Listening to the men speak outside. "Right this way, Mr. Krantz, I'll drive you to your car. Are you okay getting yourself down to the main road and to the airport?"

"Yes, I think so…" she heard Brian answered, his normally strong voice feeble with cold.

The voices faded into the distance, and then she could hear the faint sound of a car starting up.

That was when Sola released the breath she hadn't known she'd been holding. Brian was safe. In the car and on his way home. She could relax now… in the cold, dark cell she'd be calling home until spring.

"Follow me," the man in front of her said, turning to head back toward the cell's door.

"Excuse me?" she said, not understanding.

Her Russian Brute

"You would like to sleep here then?" he asked, his crystal blue eyes cutting toward the silk dog bed on the floor.

"No," she answered. "But don't I have to? Isn't that part of the deal?"

He grunted, irritation flashing across his half-damaged face.

"The *deal,* as you call it, is you stay here until spring. *Here* can be in this cage, or *here* can be in my warm house. I will let you decide."

Then he walked away, as if to say it was up to her whether she followed him or not.

Sola studied his receding back warily. Her answer should have been obvious. Of course she'd rather stay in a place with some kind of central heating. Or a fireplace at least. But…

In the end, her shivering body made the decision for her. Stiffly propelling her out of the building and into the pitch-black night before her mind had time to chime in.

The sun, which had been in the process of setting when she'd first arrived in Wolfson Point, was now completely gone. And the only reason she could see anything in front of her was because the Russian's house

70

was lit up in the distance, and the Russian was trudging slowly towards it, carrying that retro looking oil lamp.

From Sola's vantage point out there in the cold, snow-covered darkness…the stone manor looked warm and inviting.

So why was her heart beating way faster now? And why did she have the feeling that following this so-called monster into his warm house was an even more dangerous proposition than staying behind in the freezing cage?

Chapter 10

A woman opened the door as they walked up a short set of stone steps to the manor's huge back entrance.

"Name's Hannah, miss," she said as Sola followed the Russian through the door she held open for them.

"I'm Sola," she answered, a little taken aback by the smiling servant.

After meeting the beastly Russian who'd imprisoned poor Brian, she certainly hadn't expected to receive such a warm, friendly welcome to the main house.

"Well, I'm mighty pleased to meet you, Sola," Hannah answered. "There's a guest room all ready for you. Second door from the top of the stairs."

A worried pang jolted through Sola at the thought of being so near a staircase in an unfamiliar house. But at least it was warm in here, so really, she couldn't complain.

She looked around the small entryway beyond the door. It led off in two different directions. One toward a wide back staircase, and one toward a closed wooden door with the most delicious smells wafting out from behind it.

Sola's stomach grumbled, noisily reminding her she hadn't bothered to eat since her call to Lorraine at The Thirsty Wolf this morning.

This morning…wow, that seemed so long ago.

It had only been a few hours since she was nothing more than a grad student in California, wondering whether or not to press charges against her abusive ex-boyfriend.

And now…

She studied the wide back of the man who had yet to break stride as he headed toward the stairs.

And now…she was someone's prisoner.

Sola remembered what Brian had said about barely being fed during his time in the cage, and she wished like hell she hadn't been so cheap on the flight out. She should have just ordered a meal from the overpriced menu selection.

"Hannah will bring you something to eat in an hour or two," the man told her, coming to a sudden halt outside a closed door.

"Thank you," she answered politely. Even as her stomach grumbled in protest at having to wait any longer for a meal.

Apparently, the Russian could hear her stomach, too.

Her Russian Brute

"I am Russian. We eat late. But I know about you Americans and your early suppers. Hannah will make exception for you."

"You're Russian…" she repeated, remembering her question from earlier. "So are you, like, related to Alexei Rustanov? Or do all you Russians have the same sneer?"

A faint smile almost made it's way to his lips. Almost. "Alexei is my cousin."

Oh. Well, that explained it.

"Come," he said.

He pushed open the door and walked into the room, once again expecting her to follow.

She did, and was stunned to find a very cozy bedroom with an ebony four-poster bed, a dark red Berber carpet, a little red couch, and a piece of furniture she recognized as a high-backed dressing bench, thanks to the high school summer camp production of *Beauty and the Beast* she'd directed a few months ago.

The room even had a fireplace, which she imagined would do a lot to reduce the large house's nighttime chill.

As if reading her thoughts, the Russian—who had returned to the doorway, and was studying her with those crystal blue eyes—informed her, "Hannah will start a fire

74

for you when she brings your dinner. I know you Americans are not that skilled at using real fireplaces anymore."

"Ah…thank you, I guess?" she responded, not quite knowing what else to say.

And there they stood, watching each other with the same careful suspicion.

Yeah, he was definitely a Rustanov, she noted. She hadn't recognized it in the shadows of the small jailhouse, but it was easy to see now in the bright light of the bedroom. He had the same perma-sneer going as Alexei and his brother, Boris. The same high, chiseled cheekbones, too, along with that weirdly intense glitter in his eyes.

But unlike those two, this Russian's face had been through something. Something bad. Something that had presumably made him take refuge here in this remote and isolated mountain town.

"This isn't *Beauty and the Beast*," she found herself blurting out.

His crystal gaze narrowed. "What?"

"This isn't a *Beauty and the Beast*-type situation," she told him. "I'm not going to fall all over myself and sleep with you because it's winter and you can't get any more hookers up here until spring. I want to be straight with you about that."

Also, she didn't want to get used to this amazing room if she was only going to be tossed back in the freezing jail cell when she refused to put out.

A shadow crept over his face. "I understand. You want this room, but you do not wish to sleep with someone who looks like I do," he gestured towards the deeply scarred side of his face, "in order to get it."

"No!" she answered, struggling to keep her voice level. "I don't want to sleep with you because of *you*. I don't care about your face. My dad had a cleft palate—you know, a hare lip?—and he was the most beautiful person I've ever known. But you—you're ugly on the inside. Only a really messed up person would put someone over sixty years old in an unheated jail cell and then refuse to release him, even after discovering he had a very sick partner at home."

The Russian stared at her for a long time. So long, she wondered if he was trying to decide whether or not to throw her back in the cell. But then he said, "I did not know he was so old when I put him in there. Or that he had

76

a sick partner."

She shook her head. Was he serious?!

"You shouldn't have had to know that! I mean, who does that? Who locks people up in unheated cages and leaves them there for days on end with hardly anything to eat or drink?"

Again the long stare, as if he was having trouble processing her words. She wondered if maybe his English wasn't that great and she'd spoken too fast for him to follow. But she held his gaze, refusing to back down from what she'd said, even if he didn't understand all of it.

In the end, he was the one who gave in. His eyes darting away from her as he said, "If you need anything, ask Gregory or Hannah. After tonight, you can go anywhere you like. But not on full moon nights. On full moon nights, there is a strict five o'clock curfew in town, and you must stay inside."

Her eyes moved quickly from side to side before she asked the obvious question.

"Uh, what exactly happens on full moon nights?"

"It is difficult to explain, even I have trouble understanding it," he answered. "But simply put: you are not allowed to go out on these nights. It is a very important

Her Russian Brute

town rule and it must be followed."

"Okay…" she said, feeling like she'd stumbled into some kind of Beckett production. No, Pinter. No…both. This whole situation felt strange and dangerous, like the two playwrights had collaborated on a very surreal Russian performance art piece.

"And since I'm going to be living here until the spring, I guess I should ask: what's your name?"

He flinched, as if this question had taken him totally by surprise. "I am Ivan," he eventually answered. "Ivan Rustanov. Have you heard of me?"

She shook her head. "Should I have?"

He looked hard at her, sneered, and then let his eyes run over her outfit in a way that made her want to pull the lapels of Eddie's old jacket closer together over her breasts.

Usually this big jacket brought her comfort. When she wore it, she felt like she was wrapped in one of Eddie's patented bear hugs…something she really missed now that he could no longer give them. But at the moment, the jacket didn't seem to be providing nearly the amount of comfort or coverage she needed.

"Tomorrow, Hannah will take you into town for

78

more clothes. You will shop for a better coat, too, and a hat that is not silly. You will need both."

"Okay," she started to say, but was cut off when he turned and abruptly left the room.

She watched him go in a swoosh of black tailored pea coat, and felt completely baffled. By their conversation. By him. By this new and very weird set of circumstances.

Then the door slammed shut, effectively placing a barrier between the large Russian man and any of her remaining questions or comments.

* * *

I don't care about your face.

Her words continued to haunt him. Long after he'd eaten dinner. Long after his ten mile evening run on the treadmill in the home gym.

He only bothered with the nightly exercise so he'd have an easier time falling asleep. That and about a half a bottle of vodka, drunk afterwards in the main study, usually did the trick.

But that night, he was in his study and nearly a whole bottle of vodka in, and he still couldn't get her words out of his head.

Her Russian Brute

I don't care about your face.

Surely she'd been lying. But he recalled how she'd met his gaze so easily. How many woman had done that since the explosion?

Zero. Save for Boris's wife…right before she punched him during last year's Christmas dinner. And that didn't count.

No, women didn't look at him anymore. And when they did, it was nothing like it had been before. Now he most frequently saw horror mixed with pity.

But this woman had looked right at him. In the outbuilding, and in her room.

She'd looked *right* at him.

Yes, it had been with hate blazing in her eyes.

But not pity. Not pity…

I don't care about your face.

He'd been feeling so dead inside just twenty-four hours ago, but now…

Now his cock pulsed behind the zipper of his tailored pants, the newly erect flesh between his legs begging him to take it in his hand. To do what he must to get her words out of his mind.

Drinking his vodka, he rubbed himself through the

80

soft fabric. Kneading. Wanting. But not granting his body's wish.

He'd fucked his hand too much over the past year. It was something he did to stay clear headed. Tug and kill. Tug and kill. Tug and…

I don't care about your face.

But there was no one left to kill. Only her. Sleeping in the bedroom next to his. He could imagine her soft, curvy body tucked under the bed's heavy blanket. Could see himself slipping between the flannel sheets with her. Taking off those glasses, and that silly raccoon hat. Keeping her warm with his tongue between her legs, while his hands explored all the smooth, tawny brown skin he was sure to find beneath all that tweed and denim.

He'd dated a lot of tall and thin models when he'd been Ivan Rustanov, international heavyweight champion. But there was something about this woman… cute but fiery…short but big, with wide hips and thick thighs. He could almost feel those soft thighs around his waist as he drove into her, taking what he wanted without having to worry about her breaking underneath him. She was similar to his cousin's wives. The kind of woman built to take a Rustanov man.

Her Russian Brute

He'd take his time with her. *Da*, he would. He imagined himself fucking her slowly, while looking into her pretty brown eyes, no longer hidden behind glasses. And she'd look back at him. Not with pity, but with desire, because of what he was doing to her.

A hot, molten sensation startled him out of the fantasy, followed by a wet, sticky goo that he couldn't quite believe, but easily recognized from his teenage years, before being cool had trumped hormones.

He'd come in his fucking pants! Come just from thinking about her staring into his ruined face.

Come like a teenager for a woman who'd already told him she'd never sleep with him because he was ugly on the inside.

Which he was.

As the Americans would say, "Fuck my life…"

Chapter 11

Where the heck was she?

Scott shivered in the increasingly cool night. He'd been waiting on Sola's porch since the sun was high in the sky. Now it had set, and she still wasn't home.

Which had him worried. Had she gone to the police? Reported him? Jeez, that was the last thing he needed after what happened last fall. When the trashy girlfriend of a teammate hadn't taken kindly to his suggestion that she take some pride in herself and dress a little classier.

He should have just walked away when she got in his face, yelling about how no man could tell her how to dress. He should have, but he loathed mouthy women. Always had. His dad had never tolerated any backtalk from his mother, and Scott found it grating, to say the least, that so many of his teammates seemed fine letting their wives and girlfriends speak to them in such a disrespectful manner.

So he decided to teach her a lesson. He'd hit that white trash skank—just like she deserved. Just like she'd

Her Russian Brute

been asking for. And all heck had broken loose. Luckily, they'd been alone in the nightclub's unisex bathroom, so it was her word against his. But the teammate she was dating complained to upper management. And upper management got scared. It hadn't been Scott's best season, and the GM didn't want to deal with any bad press, like the sort that would happen if someone leaked the incident about Scott and that girl to the media.

In the end, it hadn't gotten out—probably because Scott was only a second-string running back. He almost never got recognized as an L.A. Sun most places he went, not unless he was with a few of the better known players. No one but that stupid girl had been hurt in the end, but unfortunately, the whole incident cast a shadow over Scott's formerly pristine reputation within the organization.

After that, Scott decided to keep his mind on the game. Telling Sola not to come down to L.A. for a while, so he could concentrate on proving his worth to his team. But then Scott missed a pass that could have sent a playoff game into overtime, and all his hard work went down the drain. As it was, when it came time to renegotiate his contract, his agent had barely been able to convince the powers-that-be to trade him instead of cutting him from the team all together.

And now Sola was nowhere to be found. Scott's heart pounded with fear. If she pressed charges, that other girl might come forward, too.

He'd seen this happen to one of his college teammates. One girl pressed rape charges against him, then other skanks started to come out of the woodwork, claiming he'd raped them, too. They were nothing but a bunch of bottom-feeders. But they'd ruined the poor guy's career. No professional organization would touch him after that, all because he took what those slutty girls were putting on display.

If Scott's football career had taught him anything, it was that the world outside Omaha was filled with big-mouthed women. Which was why getting drafted by the L.A. Suns had felt to him like being dropped into a cesspool of sin.

Finding his sweet Sola in a city full of mouthy harlots had felt like a miracle. A nice Catholic girl, and pretty to boot. She was a bit fleshier than he liked, and she insisted on living with those two faggots. But he'd been willing to put up with a few extra pounds, and he'd

85

Her Russian Brute

overlooked her living situation, since it kept her out of an even worst den of sin—those art school dormitories. He'd even forgiven her for cutting her hair, so that she looked like some kind of lesbo feminist—yet another type of degenerate found in California. After all, she'd been growing it back out ever since, and though it wasn't nearly as long as it had been when they'd first met, in a few years he'd probably forget she ever showed up at his door with that awful haircut in the first place.

He'd thought moving to Omaha—a good city with people who knew right from wrong—would be a fresh start for them. And after the rough season he'd had, he wanted nothing more than to settle down into a nice, normal life with Sola. He'd even booked a marching band as part of his proposal plan and then spent all week imagining her tears of joy when she said yes.

But she didn't say yes. In fact, she tried to break up with him. And when he'd tried to reason with her, she turned into his worst nightmare.

He shouldn't have hit her. He knew that. She obviously hadn't been thinking straight when she suggested they break up. Neither had he. For a while, he'd actually thought of letting her go after she'd proven herself

86

not to be as docile as he'd originally believed. Also, she'd publicly embarrassed him when she turned down his proposal. Real men didn't allow women to embarrass them like that.

After he hit Sola for mouthing off to him, he'd nearly walked away from the relationship altogether.

But then he'd come to his senses the morning after their fight. He'd spent over two years building a foundation for a good marriage with Sola. He had a life plan for them. He wasn't going to give up on their relationship or his plans just because she was being stubborn about his marriage proposal. That wasn't how winners operated. And no matter what the Suns told his agent, Scott knew he was a winner. He just needed to try harder with her.

He'd forgive her for what she'd said, and he'd apologize for hitting her, and they'd move on from the whole thing, just like they'd moved on from the hair episode. That's what he'd decided the morning after their fight.

So he'd driven all the way up to Valencia again with a huge bouquet of lilies…only to find it empty when he rang the doorbell. At first he'd waited patiently on the

87

concrete steps. But then after about an hour, he decided to let himself in with the key he'd secretly copied one weekend when she'd been visiting him in Los Angeles. Just to make sure she wasn't inside and ignoring his knocks.

She definitely wasn't there, but her closed laptop was parked right on top of her desk. Which meant she hadn't gone to class.

Scott opened the laptop, and almost immediately, an IM rectangle from her best friend, Anitra, popped up on the screen. *Oh, BTW, how did the break-up with the douchebag go? Did he cry?*

Acidic hatred almost cancelled out every good, peaceful feeling Scott had managed to muster up since driving up here. So *that* was why his sweet Sola had tried to break up with him! Her witch of a best friend put her up to it! He'd only met the girl once, when she'd come home to visit her family in California for the holidays, but Scott hadn't taken to her at all.

During the dinner he'd magnanimously treated her and Sola to, Anitra had spent the majority of the meal taking everything Scott said the wrong way. She'd glared at him when he expressed concern over a girl her age going to school so far from her family.

"*Women* my age do just fine on our own, thank you," she'd answered.

And she'd become downright hostile when he pointed out that it would be hard for her to find a good husband if she put in the same kind of hours as they did on those doctor shows. She'd decided she couldn't handle any of Scott's well-meaning observations, and now that she-devil was doing everything in her power to tear Sola and him apart.

Well, she wouldn't get away with it, he decided, standing up from the desk. As soon as Sola came back, he'd talk some sense into her about that best friend of hers.

He was even willing to lie if that was what it took. Girls were always fighting over guys. He'd tell Sola that Anitra had tried to come on to him behind her back, and he'd turned her down. That was why she didn't like him—because she was so jealous of everything Sola had: her beauty, her agreeableness, her lack of boastfulness—for example, Sola never went around showing off to everyone about how smart she was.

Sola would believe him. She would have to. He carefully tidied everything, like he always did when he

Her Russian Brute

checked in on her like this without her knowledge. Then he went back to the porch and waited for her to return.

But she never did, and eight hours after his arrival, his sense of determination began to sour.

Where could she be? At the police station? With another guy?

Both thoughts sent a rush of outrage through his body. She had better not have opened her mouth to anyone about their argument. That was *their* business. She'd been out of it when he left her on the living room floor yesterday, but next time he'd warn her. Just like his dad warned his mother. Opening your mouth when you weren't supposed to always came with consequences. Eventually his mom learned better than to go the authorities every time Dad got a little too rough with her. And Sola would learn, too.

These things happened. But there was no reason to bring the police into private matters.

However, as the night wore on, Scott began to relax a little. But not much. If she wasn't here, and she wasn't reporting him to the police, *where was she*?

The sound of wheels coming to a stop over concrete cut off his suspicious thoughts.

90

Sola! he thought, his heart soaring when he saw the Lexus she'd been driving the day before pull up into the driveway beside the main house.

But then the car's real owner, not Sola, got out.

"Professor Krantz!" Scott called out, jogging over to him.

"Oh, Scott. Hello." The professor said, his voice distracted as if he were in such a rush, he could barely spare three words.

"Have you seen Sola? I'm afraid we had a bit of a misunderstanding and I wanted to apologize." Scott held up the flowers as evidence of his remorse.

Brian, however, just frowned at the flowers. "What kind of misunderstanding?" he demanded, his eyes going sharp with reproach. "I saw her face, young man, and she doesn't need some barbaric football player—"

He suddenly cut himself off. "But oh dear me, why am I bothering with you? I have to go inside to Eddie and then figure out how to get us out of this mess."

"What mess? Is it something I can help with?" In Scott's experience, old people loved when you took an interest in their problems. And Sola considered this man to be like her second father, so if helping this gay guy was

Her Russian Brute

the way back into her affections…

But Brian only glared at him and said, "No, I highly doubt you could be of any help to anyone in this situation. Now, if you'll excuse me..."

Scott watched as the professor headed toward the main house's back door, then disappeared through without so much as a backwards glance at Scott.

Which meant he completely missed the murderous look on Scott's face. *Batty old faggot*, Scott thought angrily. He thought he could just dismiss him? Scott didn't think so. He'd come back here every day until Sola returned. He'd get her back, and when he did, he'd make sure she never saw that hateful witch Anitra or that faggot professor ever again.

And Sola *would* come back to him. It was only a matter of time.

Chapter 12

It was only a matter of time.

That was all Ivan could think as his body ate up another lap in the house pool. His twentieth of the day. But definitely not his last.

It was only a matter of time.

Only a matter of time before his body gave out. Only a matter of time before his mind stopped replaying her words, over and over.

He swam faster, as if the words he'd been trying not to think about were chasing after him.

I don't care about your face.

Why did her words matter? They did not—could not—matter. They were only words, after all.

But Ivan wanted her. From the moment she'd had the temerity to yell at him about his treatment of the old man, he'd wanted her in a way he hadn't wanted anyone or anything but revenge in a very long time. And six days later, he still couldn't stop thinking about her. Her compact curves, the way her eyes had blazed at him, despite her

Her Russian Brute

bruised face. Her skin, so warm and tawny. He knew she'd be soft to the touch, soft beneath his hard body…

This couldn't go on. Swimming and running, then swimming and running some more. His body, strong as it was, couldn't handle it. Neither could his mind.

He hit the slick tile wall of the pool and pushed off again, making the water churn around him.

But what could he do? She clearly hated him. The old Ivan would have taken that as a challenge. Pursued her with lavish gifts, and expensive dates—unrelenting in his chase, all the way up until the morning after he bedded her. Then he'd leave and she'd never hear from him again.

But he was no longer the old Ivan.

And more importantly, he didn't have the old Ivan's face. Negotiating her up against a wall and sweet-talking her onto his dick wouldn't work the way it used to.

Also, this woman was…different. He had to wonder if even the old Ivan would have been able to claim her. She was less than impressed with the manor house and all its perks. And she showed more interest in the town's strange full-moon curfew than anything else he'd told her.

As it was, she'd barely come out of her room all week, even going so far as to take all her meals there.

94

Hannah mentioned she'd been spending a lot of time in the solarium, but otherwise, Sola really only left her room to go down the hill to The Thirsty Wolf for an hour or so every night.

Ivan had taken to watching her leave the house from his diamond-paned study window. Though he kept swearing he wouldn't wait up for her, each night after she left, he'd somehow end up in the set of armchairs in the small alcove beneath the front entryway's main staircase, drinking the vodka he'd ordered at great cost from his homeland. Wondering if a woman, fresh and fiery as her, would find one of the town's resident males to walk her home.

But so far, every night Sola returned—alone—to Wolfson Manor around ten every night, bundled in the Lands' End jacket, gloves, winter beanie and snow boots Hannah had procured for her at the local supply store. Looking cuter and sexier than any short little brown girl in tortoiseshell glasses ought to in such an ensemble.

"Hey," she'd say when she spotted him in the front foyer with his vodka.

"Hello," he'd answer, as if he'd just happened to pick this particular place to drink his vodka and hadn't, in

Her Russian Brute

fact, been waiting up for her.

And that would be the end of their exchange. She'd walk toward the stairs. Sometimes he'd catch the faint whiff of tequila—a smell he recognized easily, since Cuervo had been one of his official sponsors when he'd been in the EFC. Then she'd climb the stairs back up to her room.

She'd only once stopped to talk to him on her very first night out.

"Since you're being so generous with the terms of my stay, could I move into one of the downstairs guestrooms?" she'd asked.

Downstairs. Away from him.

The "No" had fallen out of his mouth with all the subtlety of a brick before he'd even had a moment to wonder why she'd made the request in the first place.

She'd looked stricken, dropping her eyes and tugging at one of her ear-length curls. Which made him angry. At her, for wanting to move further from him. At himself, for caring whether she did or not.

And then he became even angrier when she tried again with, "It's just that it might make things a little easier for me. You see I—"

"How old are you?"

She blinked. "What?"

"How old are you, Sola?"

"Twenty-four," she answered carefully.

"Do you have an illness, like your teacher's spouse?"

"No, but I—"

"Then the answer is no."

Again the stunned look, as if she were trying to process his cruelty. Which was quickly followed by a look of resignation, as if she were used to cruel people. "Okay, well…"

She started for the stairs.

"What happened to your face?" he'd asked her.

She raised a hand to her bruised cheek, as if only now remembering how bad it looked. "I…it's a long story."

He'd stared at her for a moment. Then said, "I would like to hear this long story, Sola."

She shrugged. "Yeah, well, I'm tired, and apparently we're not trying to be pals right now, so I'm going to bed. It's been a long day."

That was the lengthiest conversation they'd had so

Her Russian Brute

far. But he'd waited up for her every night since. And every night, he'd watch her clump up the stairs in her snow boots and shut herself back in her room after her nightly trip to the town bar. No words of greeting, just a look of grim determination on her face. Like she was serving out a prison sentence, which made him feel even more like a head case for wanting her as badly as he did—

He stopped suddenly, moving into a strong tread in the middle of the pool. That tingling sensation was back. The feeling he was being watched. It had happened at least once or twice a day since Sola's arrival. Usually when he was in the pool.

But whenever he stopped to look at the narrow band of windows off the long hallway at the front of the house, no one was there. Maybe it was just his imagination, but...

I don't care about your face.

"Sir?"

Ivan started, splashing himself in the face. He took a moment to wipe the water from his eyes to find Gregory standing at the far edge of the pool.

"Yes, what is it?" he asked testily, wondering if he'd merely been sensing Gregory. Not Sola, the pretty young woman who didn't care about his face.

98

"It's nearly four, sir, and I wanted to remind you it's a full moon night."

Yes, another damn full moon night. He'd nearly forgotten about the town's bizarre custom with their unexpected visitor now in residence. The entire town took off the full twenty-four hours of each full moon night every month—from sunrise to sunrise—with a hard curfew of 5:00 PM. According to Gregory, it was a very old tradition. One that dated back to when the town first began as a small Native American hunting village in the 1500s. Eventually, the village was taken over by a large extended family of white settlers—"the Wolfson line," as Gregory referred to them—in the 1800s.

"Hannah will, of course, leave dinner for you and Sola in the kitchen," Gregory told him. "Perhaps Miss Sola would like to join you tonight in the dining room, seeing as how Hannah won't be able to deliver a plate to her room? Also, should I remind her not to go down to The Thirsty Wolf this evening?"

"Yes, yes," Ivan agreed. "I'll talk to her about dinner and tell her she can't go to The Thirsty Wolf tonight."

"Ah, maybe I ought to convey the message about dinner to her along with a friendly reminder about the

Her Russian Brute

town curfew?" Gregory answered, his tone worried.

Ivan narrowed his eyes, not liking what the older man was insinuating. Clearly he thought Ivan didn't have enough charm in his arsenal to get a woman with no other meal options for the night, to have dinner with him.

"No, I will do it," he repeated more firmly. He swam quickly to the side of the pool and lifted himself up and out. His arms screamed in protest, not appreciating the sudden movement after the workout he'd put them through.

But at least his erection was gone.

"Where is she?" he asked the older man, toweling himself off.

"In the solarium, sir, but perhaps—"

He didn't give Gregory the chance to finish, just threw on his black terry cloth robe and headed toward the back of the house.

Chapter 13

Ivan found her in the solarium, just as Gregory had said. Since this room received the most sun in the house, he'd expected to find her curled up in a seat. Reading, or playing a game on her phone. The house didn't having any televisions…the reception was non-existent up here in the mountains. Same for Wi-Fi. So reading, exercising, and playing games were pretty much the only available activities unless you had a job to keep you occupied.

No wonder Thompson Wolfson had opted out of spending his winters here, choosing instead to gamble away the months in places like Vegas.

But Sola wasn't up to anything nearly so quiet. When he walked in the room, Ivan was hit by a wall of sound. Opera, he realized, after the singer belted out a few bars. But it definitely wasn't the kind of opera he'd had to struggle to stay awake through in the past. This music was backed by synthesizers that sounded like sci-fi laser guns blasting in the background.

If that wasn't strange enough, Sola was in the middle

of the large room, moving from place to place with each bar sung. Turning this way and that while lip-synching, as if testing out the various positions.

He watched her bemusedly for a few seconds until she turned and spotted him standing in the doorway. She yelped and then her mouth moved with words he couldn't hear. He tilted his head to the side and shook his head, mouthing, "Too loud!"

She scurried over to the sound system he'd never bothered to use and switched the music off.

But it was still ringing in his ears when she asked, "Hey, what's up? What are you doing here?"

All of the bruising had faded from her face now, and even though she wasn't wearing any make-up, he was struck by her prettiness. It was like she was lit up from the inside with a kind of light he'd never known.

He folded his arms across his massive chest, to keep himself from following through on the compulsion to reach out and remove her glasses. "The question is, what are you doing here?" he returned, voice terse with restraint.

"What?! Oh wait, hold on…" She reached up and pulled two orange foam earplugs from her ears. "Forgot I had these in."

He lifted his good eyebrow. She'd come here from California with just the clothes on her back and, apparently, a pair of earplugs. He was beginning to realize this woman had very strange priorities.

"What exactly were you doing?" he asked again.

"Oh, I'm…practicing, I guess you'd say. I'm a directing grad when I'm not serving time as a prisoner by proxy. I'm trying to figure out as much blocking for my thesis production as I can, so I can hit the ground running when I go back to school in the spring."

An unfamiliar sensation assailed him. The thought of her not being able to complete her studies because of the bargain they'd struck didn't sit well with him. And he shifted from foot to foot, feeling the oddest compulsion to apologize.

"So you're here, because…?" she prompted.

She didn't meet his eyes as she asked this question, he noticed. Instead, she looked around the room, as if trying to find something to get her out of even this small conversation with him.

But he wanted her direct gaze. The one she'd given him that first night when she looked at his face and into his

103

Her Russian Brute

eyes without flinching. So he tried again.

"You are directing opera in the spring?" he asked in his best, most clear English. "Is it a new work? I've never heard this before."

That did it. Her face lit up and she gave him her full attention.

"Yes! It's a new work. Set in space. So, I guess you could say it's literally a space opera. One of the writing grads in the playwriting program wrote the script, and it's brilliant. I already know exactly who to cast in it, and I've been working with a production designer on the set. Hopefully if I do enough groundwork, I won't be too far behind when I return to school."

He wondered if she had any idea how cute she looked when she did that. Thought aloud, with her whole face scrunched up, her eyes widening and narrowing with excitement.

"Are you an opera fan?" she asked.

"No," he answered, before remembering his old rules about telling women exactly what they wanted to hear in order to get them into bed. Before he could keep the light from dying on her face.

"Oh."

104

"It's just that I've seen too much of it. My family had a box at our local opera house in St. Petersburg, and I was made to attend every production from the age of six."

"Well, that sounds really messed up," she said with a teasing lift of her dark eyebrows. "I can tell you had a really hard childhood. Box seats at the opera, wow…"

A hot fizz of anger bubbled in his head. He didn't like being dismissed by her. Or being made to feel like a spoiled brat.

Even if it was true.

"I think rich and poor alike can agree opera is sometimes boring."

"Not the way I'm going to stage it," she answered with a grin. "My thesis is all about making opera accessible and interesting. And finding ways to keep production costs down, so regular people can attend. Maybe even with children."

He shook his head, having never met a woman so passionate about her future plans. "Why does bringing opera to the common people excite you so much?" he asked, truly wanting to know.

In his experience, opera attendance was often used to further set the rich apart from the poor. Box seats and season tickets were a luxury only the wealthiest could afford in Russia, and he assumed it was the same here in America. He recalled seeing a few scruffy-looking individuals in the standing-room only section from his box seat vantage point, but the majority of opera attendees in Russia were from the same social strata as him.

She started to reply but stopped.

"Like you really care," she muttered, dropping her gaze away from him.

"But—"

"Did you come in here for a reason or what? I'm kind of in the middle of something…"

Hostile words, but then her gaze drifted slowly down his body. And Ivan found himself responding to the heat that flared in her eyes before she quickly looked away.

He stepped closer. Liking the way it felt to have a woman look at him again with raw interest. Especially since he was interested in her. Very, very interested.

"I came here to tell you something, Sola," he said, his voice sounding hoarse even to his own ears. He cleared his throat and retried, threading his voice with a little more authority as he informed her, "Hannah and Gregory have the night off for the full moon holiday. You will eat the dinner Hannah has made for us with me in the kitchen."

"Ah…" He watched her throat work up and down as she swallowed. "No, thank you."

"It is not a request," he informed her.

"Well, it should have been. So, no. I won't."

She carefully stepped away from him.

And he very intentionally stepped closer to her, invading her personal space the way he used to when he was in the habit of challenging and fighting grown men.

Of course he'd never put his hands on Sola. At least not with the intention of hurting her.

But he had the same feeling he used to get when he threw the first punch in the ring, when he said, "You have been watching me. Every day you watch me swim, but yet you refuse to have dinner with me."

Sola's face fell, and she suddenly looked very flustered.

"Yes…I mean, no…I mean, I haven't been…" She took a deep steadying breath. "Look, Hannah and Gregory have the night off and you're telling me to have dinner with you and I'm saying no. Because I don't want to. Not with you."

"Because of my face," he sneered. "You are

107

Her Russian Brute

attracted to my body, but my face repels you..."

"No," she replied, her tone tight as a drawn string. "Your face has nothing to do with it. It's still your attitude. Because guess what, I've been attending a really expensive art school in California for the last four and a half years, and I've had enough of spoiled trust fund babies to last me a lifetime."

"You think me spoiled and petty?" he said angrily. Then he did the opposite of what one should do when an opponent lands a good, solid blow: Ivan panicked and swung wildly.

"Well, you are judgmental and bitchy. And the kitchen will be closed to you unless you agree to eat with me. I will lock it."

"Okay, cool," she answered with a disgusted shake of her head. "Well, I guess you just proved my point."

Frustration cut a bitter path across his chest, tugging his lips up into yet another sneer. He had no idea how to handle a woman like this. It should have been relatively easy. Clearly she liked his body, and he was dying to find out what was hidden beneath that oversized tweed jacket she always wore and those glasses. They'd be stuck together in this house all winter. He wanted her. And she

108

wanted him. He could tell. As it stood, they should have been fucking like bunnies for the last few days, at least.

Yet she couldn't even bring herself to share a meal with him.

"You are here in this house, and not in a cell, because I allow it," he said. "You will eat when I say you will eat. And I say you will eat dinner with me at six o'clock, like early-eating Americans."

He realized immediately after he spoke that he must have been be truly angry. Not only because of the nastiness of his tone, but also because he was dropping articles and betraying his impeccable English education. He sounded like nothing more than a caricature of a Russian immigrant speaking heavily accented, broken English.

"Oh I see. And if I refuse, do you want me to go back to the cell?" she asked, her tone sounding quite serious. "Can I at least get my coat first, or are you taking that away, too?"

He stared down at her for a few long moments. Seething.

Then with a noise somewhere between a yell and a growl, he turned away, no longer able to trust himself to

Her Russian Brute

stay in this room with her for a second longer. Lest he say something else, something she'd use to further prove her point about him being like the spoiled rich kids she went to school with. One who didn't deserve to have dinner with her, let alone touch her.

Ivan had conquered men. Both inside the ring and out. Countless men had resorted to begging beneath his unrelenting fists. Yet he was unable to handle one woman...a girl, really.

So he left. All the while wondering what disturbed him more. That he couldn't figure out how to get Sola into his bed...

...or that every word she'd said about him was 100% true.

Chapter 14

Sola fumed long after Ivan left her alone in the solarium. Mainly because he'd been right. She *had* been watching him swim. But only for a little while, just a few furtive moments, when she thought he couldn't see her. But obviously he had seen her.

After today's little peep show, she hadn't expected him to show up in the solarium—where she'd been trying desperately to distract herself from thoughts of her sexy captor.

And seriously, could he have looked any sexier? she wondered, with an inner groan. She'd thought he'd been something to watch when he was swimming, muscles rippling as his strong body sliced through the water like a knife through butter. But up close and personal? In an open robe and in tight black swim trunks, water dripping down his torso toward his heavily yoked waist…

She'd barely been able to hide her reaction to him. Prattling on about opera, afraid to meet his gaze, lest hers accidentally stray down that magnificent body.

Her Russian Brute

A magnificent body she definitely should NOT want. *You know, because of the whole he locked your mentor, an elderly man with a sick husband, in a jail cell and then basically forced you to stay here against your will thing?* she reminded herself snidely.

What had Brian called him? A brute—yes, he was a brute, she reminded herself as she stomped up the stairs to her room. She'd meant every word she'd said about him being a spoiled brat...and she had no idea why she couldn't stop thinking about him.

With a frustrated huff, she grabbed her coat off the bed and headed back downstairs. So determined was she to show him he wasn't the boss of her, she had her coat zipped up and the Thermalite gloves she'd stored in its pockets on her hands before she even reached the front door.

Stupid Russian brute, she thought, marching angrily down the hill. Trying to call her out for ogling him. Trying to use food as a way to get her into his bed. Well, she'd show him. Hannah's food was great, but she'd been meaning to try that lamb stew at The Thirsty Wolf all week, anyway.

Yet when Sola walked through the bar's main

112

entrance, she found Lorraine there, alone.

That's odd, she thought to herself, frowning. Even stranger, Lorraine was placing what appeared to be a large iron door against the wall where the bottles were shelved. At least the large rectangle with hinges looked like it was made of iron. But it couldn't possibly be because as tough as Lorraine was, she would never have had the strength to lift something that heavy at her age. However it sure looked like that was exactly what she was doing.

Suddenly, the older woman stopped her work and sniffed the air. Then she quickly turned, her eyes widening when she saw Sola standing just inside the door.

"Sola? What are you doing here?!"

"Um, I was hoping to get a bowl of lamb stew," Sola answered as her eyes continued to scan the rest of the room. Not only was the main bar empty—and it was *never* empty, at least not that she'd ever seen—but all the metal chairs in the dining area had been placed upside down on the round, wooden tables. Even weirder, the chairs were strung through with what looked like some sort of very thin, silver chain. It was as if someone had taken a delicate silver necklace and threaded it through the backs of each chair. But why? Sola wondered.

Her Russian Brute

"We're closed on full moon nights, Sola. Everything is," Lorraine's voice rang out across the bar, interrupting her confused observations.

"Oh yeah…" She'd completely forgotten about the full moon night rule, despite Ivan reminding her about it earlier in the solarium.

Sola once again cursed her Russian captor. There was no way she would have forgotten about the curfew if he hadn't made her so angry.

"Hannah didn't make you dinner tonight?" Lorraine asked, her tone agitated, bordering on bewildered.

"She did," Sola quickly assured the perturbed bar keep. "But…"

She trailed off, not quite knowing how to explain that thanks to an argument with her captor, she'd been shut out of the house's kitchen.

Lorraine didn't seem all that interested in her explanations. "It's after five o'clock, Sola! Far as I can tell, there is no reason for you to be wandering around town after curfew." Her arms were crossed in front of her chest, her expression stern and almost parental.

"I'm sorry, Lorraine. I know I shouldn't be out, but…" Sola trailed off again because truth be told, she

114

hadn't really thought it would be a big deal if she bent the rules a little. Gregory and Hannah had been rather vague when she asked for more details about the full moon nights. Just a bunch of stuff about traditions and the original tribe who settled here hundreds of years ago.

But again, Lorraine didn't give Sola time to ruminate further.

"Look, the full moon could rise any minute now," she told Sola, with something that sounded an awful lot like panic wobbling her normally strong voice. "I've got to get down to the basement. I could—" she cleared her throat. "I could get in trouble for harboring someone after curfew."

She could get in trouble? What?

"Lorraine," she started.

But the older woman was already backing away toward the iron door.

"I've got to go," she said, again. "But I'll call Hannah and Gregory first thing in the morning. You stay here—do not leave—until they come to get you. Help yourself to anything in the kitchen. I think I have a few blankets in the office for you to sleep on. But do *not* open this door. And do *not* open the front door, either. Keep it

Her Russian Brute

locked. No matter what you hear. Remember, Hannah or Gregory will come round to get you first thing in the morning."

"First thing in the morning?!? Wait, what?!?! I don't understand. Lorraine, wait!"

But it was too late. The older woman had disappeared through the heavy metal door with an echoing slam. The next thing Sola heard was the clicking and sliding sounds of locks engaging.

"Lorraine?" she called out. "Lorraine?!"

No answer, just the fading thumps of feet descending the basement stairs, faster than she would have thought a woman Lorraine's age could move.

What the...?

Seriously confused, Sola stood in the now silent bar, trying to decide what to do. Lorraine had been adamant that she not leave the premises until the next morning. But Sola honestly had no idea why Lorraine expected her to wait here all night for someone to pick her up when she'd been walking herself home for a week now with no problem whatsoever. And there was no way she was going to spend all night at The Thirsty Wolf, waiting for someone from the house to get her the next day.

116

Mind made up, Sola opened the main door and walked out into the cold evening. She slowly began to head back up the town's main road, then up the hill towards the manor. The return walk was a lot slower going. Not only because it was uphill, but because the wind was blowing directly in her face. Filling her eyes with tears and pushing her back, almost as if it didn't want her to reach the house.

Or maybe the weather was just a reflection of her mood. She didn't much feel like going back to the house. It was nearly six o'clock and her stomach was grumbling loudly. She could just picture Ivan in the kitchen. Eating the delicious meal Hannah had prepared. Gloating, because she'd be going to bed hungry.

Plus, she wouldn't be able to have her usual nightcap, which in her state, might bring on all kinds of troubles after she went to bed.

God, she hated whining. She'd learned a long time ago to accept that the world wasn't fair. But she'd never come as close to feeling sorry for herself as she did right now, fighting the bitterly cold wind in an attempt to return to the manor-shaped jail cell—

A low growl interrupted her troubled thoughts, and

she snapped her head around. Was that a dog? She peered carefully into the surrounding trees until she spotted a large shape just a few feet away from where she stood.

No, not a dog. This animal was way bigger. Maybe a wolf? It had a pair of green eyes that seemed to glow under the light of the full moon. For some reason that she could only chalk up to fear-based delusions, the eyes put her in mind of Gregory. But these eyes definitely weren't kind like Gregory's. Especially considering they were paired with a fierce, growling muzzle.

Sola tried backing away slowly. The house was only a few meters from where she stood. Close, but in the deep snow, so far away...

Did she dare risk making a run for it?

She didn't have time to ponder her predicament for very long. The wolf suddenly advanced towards her, it's teeth bared threateningly.

And Sola made up her mind in less than a split second: she screamed and ran. As fast as her snow boots could carry her. Faster than she'd ever run before, thanks, in part, to the massive boost of fear-based adrenaline that shot through her nervous system.

Not fast enough though. She could feel the wolf at

her back. Closing the distance between them a heck of a lot faster than she was closing the distance between herself and the door.

But then the manor's front door suddenly flung open, bathing the dark scene in light as a massive figure sprinted toward her.

"No, no!" she screamed, when she realized what Ivan planned to do.

But it was too late. The wolf was in mid-air, leaping toward her, but instead of sinking it's teeth into her back, it collided with Ivan.

Sola watched in wide-eyed horror as the Russian caught the wolf by the throat mid-leap, and punched it. Yes, punched it. Once. Twice. Then a third time.

What. The. Good. Jesus. Her brain was still having a hard time computing what she just saw, even as she watched the gray wolf fall to the ground, knocked out cold.

Then Ivan was grabbing her by the arm. "Come, Sola!" he yelled, yanking her back toward the house.

Somewhere in the distance, another wolf growled. And beyond that, multiple wolves began howling repeatedly. Their eerie cries intermingling and sending

Her Russian Brute

twin jolts of fear and awe up her spine.

I'm coming, Russian dude. You don't have to ask me twice!

Sola was, for once, incredibly happy to follow wherever the Russian brute led.

Chapter 15

"So, I stand corrected," Sola said about ten minutes later, as she poured some of Ivan's expensive vodka onto a washcloth. "This *is* a little bit like *Beauty and the Beast*."

She came to stand in front of the entryway's armchair, where Ivan was currently seated. Such a pretty sight to behold—until she pressed the vodka-saturated cloth onto the ugly mark on Ivan's chest where the wolf had scratched him.

"Ow!" he yelled, as the alcohol burned into the wound.

"Including the part where you whine like a baby while I try to patch you up," Sola grumbled.

He sensed she was only complaining because she was still in a state of shock. Once the door slammed behind him, she'd spent nearly a full minute trembling before noting his ripped shirt and saying, "It scratched you. Oh my gosh, it scratched you. We have to fix that!"

She'd pushed him into the armchair, and then burst into a whirlwind of nerve-fueled activity. He'd watched

Her Russian Brute

her search the house for a medical kit. When she couldn't find one, her eyes fixed on the half-empty bottle of vodka next to his usual chair.

"This will have to do," she muttered to herself.

Ivan had admired her resourcefulness. But even now, for all her snarky comments, her hands still trembled as she applied the damp cloth to the large scratch.

Still, there was a difference between understanding why she was being snarky in the wake of the wolf attack, and tolerating it.

He glowered at her. "I have never seen this movie, *Beauty and the Beast*, but I would not need patching up if you had not gone off by yourself on a full moon night."

Instead of getting upset, however, she squinted at him with a quizzical smile. "Are you sure you haven't seen it? Because that line is totally in the movie."

He huffed in frustration. "Are you done yet?"

Sola stepped back with a frown. "Yeah, I guess I am. I can't find so much as a single Band-Aid in this house, so that's pretty much all I can do. But we need to figure out how to cover up that wound. Wait, I think I saw some duct tape in the cleaning supply closet."

And that was how he found himself fighting off an

erection as he watched Sola cover the nasty looking scratch with a dry wash cloth and two lengths of duct tape.

"This is going to hurt like a bitch when it comes off," she half-apologized when she'd finished applying the makeshift bandage. "But it's better than taking the chance of it getting infected before we can get you to the town clinic tomorrow."

"I will not need clinic," he said, rising to a stand. "Scratch is not so deep."

"But—"

"If you will excuse me, I will go to bed now. It has been a very long night."

"Oh, okay, you're going to bed. Okay…" Her words were agreeable enough, but he sensed disappointment behind them.

"Would you like me to stay up with you?" Then he thought of all his cousin's wives, and their touchy-feely ways. "Do you need a hug?" he asked her.

"No! Oh, gosh, no," she said. "Of course not. I'd never ask for something like that from you."

"Because of *my attitude*," he said, paraphrasing her earlier words.

"No—" she cut off, obviously frustrated. "You

123

know, I'm a really good communicator," she informed him. "Actors and techs love me, but with you, I always feel like I'm saying the wrong thing."

Funny, he felt the exact same way. But he waited for her to finish, wondering where she was going with this.

"I only meant I don't want to keep you up. That's all. No judgment or bitchiness or anything. I just think you deserve a good night's sleep after you, you know, punched—I mean actually *punched out a wolf* to save me. So um, yeah…definitely, definitely go to bed. And um… thank you."

She stood on her tiptoes and before he could think to stop her, pressed her lips into the side of his face. The ruined side of his face.

He thought he'd been hard before, but her kiss turned his cock into a piece of stone. It ached so painfully between his legs, he had to make himself go completely still for fear of mauling her.

And maybe she felt it too, because her eyes widened a little before she stepped away from him and said, "Yeah…soooo…I think I'll head upstairs now. First thing tomorrow, I'll run into town and get you some bandages for that cut. And while we're on this topic, what kind of

124

place doesn't have any first aid supplies? I mean, this is ridiculous!"

"You do not have to do that."

"Do what? Oh, you mean the bandages?" She shot him a look of exasperation. "Look. Cut the macho guy crap, okay? I want to do it. I mean, it's the least I can do."

Sola turned and walked to the stairs before he could argue with her any further. "Good night!" she called down to him, as she ran up the steps.

Ivan didn't answer. Nor did he move. For a very long time after she left, he remained rooted to the spot. Finding it hard to breathe.

* * *

Supermodels had shown up without invitation to his after-fight parties and sucked him off passionately as if paying him his due. Groupies in matching lingerie often appeared at his penthouse hotel rooms, seemingly out of nowhere, like so much erotic magic. Back when he'd been Ivan Rustanov, EFC champion, there'd been a constant stream of lovely women. So many, he could barely remember their faces and he certainly couldn't recall more than one or two names.

Yet he couldn't sleep for thinking of the kiss one girl

had pressed to his cheek. And his daily battle of trying not to wank-off while thinking of her was lost late that night when, after hours of tossing and turning, he flipped onto his back and pushed the covers down with a resigned grunt.

Thoughts of her curvy body sizzled through his brain as he reached under the band of his silk boxers and took himself in hand. What would she feel like beneath all those clothes? Soft, so soft, he imagined. He could almost feel the press of her full thighs around his waist as he thrust into her, and the mental image of him taking one of her beautiful breasts in his mouth very nearly shorted out his brain.

This line of thinking was enough to produce a few drops of pre-cum, making his job easier as his palm moved up and down his rigid shaft—

The click of the door opening froze his hand in mid-motion. He was about to yell at Gregory for coming in without knocking when he realized two things:

One: Gregory was off tonight.

And, two…

Gregory wasn't standing at the door. But Sola was.

The room was heavily shadowed, but his captive,

dressed in a long flannel nightgown that Hannah must have bought for her, was partially illuminated by the light of the full moon streaming through the large picture window.

"My feet are cold," she said, her voice sleepy and sweet and tinged with a very faint accent he'd never heard in it before. "You have a fire in here."

He frowned, watching her glide toward his fireplace, holding her hands out in front of her even though his hearth was as cold and devoid of a fire as hers. Gregory hadn't been there to light it, and Ivan, being Russian and accustomed to cold winters, didn't really need the extra warmth of the fire to sleep.

But then she stopped. Looked at him frozen in the bed, his motionless hand fisted around his cock. He realized the moonlight must have shown him to her as clearly as it was showing her to him, because she asked, "What are you doing?"

"I am…" he didn't finish. Couldn't finish. Could only stare.

And she stared right back, eyes unblinking behind her glasses.

Then she surprised the hell of out him by saying,

Her Russian Brute

"Keep going," her voice barely above a whisper. "I want to watch you…"

The moonlight reflected off her glasses as she moved closer to the bed. "Please keep going."

He did. Stroking himself slowly under her curious gaze. Discovering in that moment that he didn't have the willpower to deny this woman…

"Mmm…" she said, watching him intently. "That turns me on so bad. So bad…"

She bunched up the skirt of her nightgown with one hand, and he nearly spilled right then and there when her other hand started moving between her legs.

"No, don't stop," she said when his hand fell away from his throbbing erection. "Keep going."

"I can't, Sola. The sight of you. It is too much for me to bear without coming too quickly. Like school boy."

"Oh," she said, hand falling away from her pussy in disappointment. But then she brightened and said, "In that case, can we have sex? I really want to have sex with you, Ivan. It's pretty much all I've been thinking about…"

Not waiting for an answer, she advanced on the bed. And only muscle memory alone made it possible for Ivan to reach into the nearby drawer and grab a condom. Even so, he barely got himself sheathed before she was climbing on top of him, guiding his steel-hard cock toward the heat of her entrance.

He'd done countless things with countless girls before her. Pussy had come so easily back then. Yet the simple act of her easing her wet, hot pussy onto his straining dick nearly blanked his mind. And he thanked the fighting gods for the discipline Boris had instilled in him, because his physical self-control was the only thing that kept him from blowing his load right then and there.

"So big. Even bigger than I imagined," she gasped out, her hands splayed across his chest. She started riding him with a moan. As if she'd been dreaming about this. Waiting for this. Just as he had.

"Oh, fuck, that's good," she moaned. "So good, Ivan."

He'd never heard her curse before, even at her angriest. And the filthy word following from her bowed mouth did something to him. Turned him on so bad, he had to close his eyes against the sight of her. Close his eyes and think of the most boring things possible: opera, winding sports tape around his hands, burpee drills. He'd been dead inside for so long before this moment, but now

Her Russian Brute

he was dangerously aroused and having to resort to the tricks of his youth to keep from coming too quickly. As she ground herself on top of him, he could do little more than lie there, his whole body tense with the fight to stay there with her and not come too soon.

However, his white-knuckled fight was abruptly lost when she arched forward and kissed him. Control became impossible then, and every part of his body rushed to fulfill his own greedy desire. His hands found her silky curls, his hips rolling up into her faster and faster with a mind of their own. And his mouth…he inhaled her, swallowing her kiss whole, as he entwined her tongue with his.

Thank God their first kiss unhinged her, too. She soon became like a maniac on top of him, hips grinding and grinding, until just a few moments later when she came with a helpless scream as his hard mouth plundered her much softer one. Her pussy milking him so wet and hot, he immediately flooded the condom with the load he'd been holding back for days and days. From the very first moment he'd met her.

She giggled against his lips as they came down from the orgasm together.

"Ohhhh, that was even better than I thought it would be, Ivan," she told him in a soft sing-song voice. "So fucking good…"

She rubbed her face into the ruined side of his, like a cat saying thank you. Then she said, "My feet are warm now. Good night."

With that, she climbed off of him and left the room without another word, the door clicking closed behind her. If not for the distinct smell of sex in the room, he would have thought she'd been a dream. Maybe even a hallucination.

But he could still smell her on his skin. Still feel her there, too. Even after he showered the next morning, reluctantly washing off her scent. He'd been lackadaisical about his hygiene regimen in the years since the bomb. But that morning, his desire not to smell the next time he saw her won over his desire to capture what had happened between them.

However, he needn't have bothered with a morning shower. Like the rest of the town, she didn't come out of her room all morning. He found himself lingering in his vodka chair, pretending to read a book about Nikola Tesla while he waited for her to emerge.

Her Russian Brute

But she never did, and finally he retired to the study, deciding he needed a drink of vodka even earlier than usual. Just a few moments after his first pour, Hannah showed up at his study door with a large bandage.

"Sola said you might be in need of this, sir. I had the town nurse look for one and bring it up to the house as soon as I heard."

"It was only a small scratch," he answered. But he took the bandage from Hannah, who continued to eye him warily, despite the fact that he'd nearly forgotten about the scratch in the first place. He'd removed that silly bandage Sola had made for him less than a minute after going up to his own bedroom, and he hadn't thought much about the wound since.

"You saw her?" he asked, curious to hear news of the woman who'd come to him last night but hadn't come out of her room all day.

"Yes, I just checked in on her and she told me all about the wolf attack." Hannah wrung her hands. "Are you *sure* you're all right, sir?"

He shrugged. "Yes, I am fine."

"And it was just a scratch?" Hannah asked worriedly. "Not a bite? You're sure?"

"*Da*, just a scratch, but thank you for the bandage. Was Sola okay—I mean, after the attack?"

Hannah frowned at the change of subject. "She seems fine, sir. Tired, and she mentioned being hungry, but then she said I should check with you first. Something about you banning her from the kitchen?"

His brows pulled low. Did she really believe that ban was still in place after what they'd shared last night? The thought of her not eating all day tore at his heart.

"No, I did not mean—it was a misunderstanding between us. You can bring her a meal. That is fine. Of course it is fine. "

Hannah started to go, but then turned back to tell him, "And by the way, my mate—I mean, Gregory—is feeling a little under the weather today. I hope you don't mind him taking a sick day. I know we never discussed that before…"

"It is fine," he answered, before she could continue.

But still Hannah fretted in his study doorway.

"Are you sure you're fine, sir? Maybe you should let me take a look at that wound…"

"I am fine," he insisted, voice brooking no argument. "But I *am* hungry."

Her Russian Brute

Hannah looked like she wanted to say something more, but at the last second, she demurred. "Yes, of course, sir. I'll go whip something up. Right away."

Presumably Hannah brought them both dinner, but Sola remained in her room, nothing but the sound of opera streaming out of it to let him know she was still there.

He thought about knocking on her door, asking her...

That's where his mind stuttered. What exactly did he want to ask her about? The fact that they'd had sex last night and she'd yet to come out of her room to—do what, exactly? Acknowledge it? Kiss him? Reassure him, like he was a weak, insecure man? He thought of all the good girls he'd claimed, tentatively asking, as he sat on the edges of their beds, if they would see him again. If this was more than a one-night stand.

He'd had a standard response for questions like that back then: "We had fun tonight. We will see about tomorrow." Even though he'd already known the answer to their timid questions. *Da*, this was definitely a one-night stand. There were too many girls in this world in need of fucking to end up stuck with just one.

That had been his reasoning back then, but now...

134

Theodora Taylor

Now… it felt like he'd give anything to have Sola come out of her room and tell him last night had meant something to her. That what they'd done together had not only taken over her body, but also her heart. Even if only a little.

That she felt the same way he did. That she couldn't stop thinking about what they'd done together, how well they'd fit together, moved together…he wanted to hear her say what happened last night had felt like a miracle to her, too.

But she never left her room. And he'd ended up right back in the pool that evening. Swimming off his frustration. Followed by another session of tossing and turning in his bed. Trying to convince himself not to beat off to the memory of her, since apparently it really had only been a one-night stand.

He'd almost given up on ever falling asleep again, when his door opened.

"Hi, my feet are cold," Sola said in the doorway. "Can we have sex?"

The answer to that was yes. Of course.

He welcomed her back into his bed, throwing off the covers as she climbed on top of his body. All the while

135

Her Russian Brute

wondering what a monster like him had done to deserve a miracle like her.

Chapter 16

Six days after the night of the wolf attack, Sola woke up just like she'd been waking up every morning since that harrowing experience…happy, with a sore pussy, and wearing her glasses.

The happiness she had no explanation for. She was in the same situation she'd been in since she'd arrived at this house, but now she didn't even have The Thirsty Wolf to distract her. She was way too scared to leave the house at night after getting attacked by that wolf. And it wasn't like she could always count on being saved by her Russian captor.

Which brought her to the issue of the soreness. She'd obviously been sleep masturbating. Again. And though she'd had no proof that this latest round of masturbation had been brought on by the man who'd accused her of watching him six nights ago, she knew he had to be the reason she kept waking with her sex and breasts throbbing and sore. Because of him, she must have spent most of the night with one hand deep in her pussy,

Her Russian Brute

and the other groping her own breasts.

And it wasn't the first time this had happened. Scott had once angrily shaken her awake in the middle of the night after her loud moans woke him from a deep sleep. She'd obviously been pleasuring herself after a less than satisfying session with him.

It had been a pretty messed up way to have your boyfriend find out you have a sleep disorder. And she'd had to think fast to come up with a plausible excuse. She told him she'd wanted him again, and hadn't realized what she was doing. She pointed out that if she hadn't been in a state of animated sleep, instead of putting on her glasses and pleasuring herself, she would have just reached over and asked him to have sex with her again.

Well, maybe...

Truthfully, as appealing as Scott was on paper— perfect face, perfect smile, perfect body—he left a lot to be desired in the bedroom. It was always missionary-style with no talking whatsoever. He didn't believe in oral, and he only fingered her until she got wet enough for him to slip inside.

He had a pretty low sex drive anyway, often treating sex like something he needed to check off his to do list.

Like: fifteen bicep curls, fifteen push-ups, fifteen minutes of sex with Sola. Afterwards, he'd usually turn on the TV and watch a movie—like there, that's over with, now let's reward ourselves for a job well done!

Scott had some different notions about sex. That they shouldn't do it too much until they got married, because it really should be reserved for what nature intended: making babies. But he was also a man, he'd explained to her when he first introduced the subject of her taking birth control so they could take their formerly chaste—at his insistence—relationship to the next level. And he already knew she was the girl for him—even if they'd both given their virginity to others in what he'd called the "indiscretions of youth."

So they'd begun a sexual relationship consisting of conventional sex with a little fingering to warm her up. It rarely ended in an orgasm for Sola unless she was super horny, but she'd accepted the situation for what it was. Mostly because she'd only been in her very early twenties when they'd first met. She'd been young and naïve and completely stunned that a pro football player would choose her, lowly Marisol Carillo, to be his girlfriend. Also, as they say: cold pizza is better than no pizza.

Her Russian Brute

To Sola, who'd never had a serious boyfriend before Scott, it hadn't seemed like too much to put up with. And though sex with him could be frustrating at times, she could usually hold out until he fell asleep at which point she would sneak into her bathroom with the battery operated boyfriend she kept hidden there in a drawer. Or if she were staying at his place, she'd tide herself over with a glass or two of wine to ensure a deep, undisturbed sleep. But the night she woke Scott with her moaning, she'd fallen asleep in front of the TV before she remembered to have her nightcap.

And that mistake resulted in the second biggest argument she and Scott ever had. *No*, she thought, remembering their last and final fight with a wince. *Make that the third biggest.*

Anitra had seen right through him from the very beginning. "I don't care what everyone else says," she said after that one disastrous dinner. "You deserve a hell of a lot better."

Back then, she'd just folded her arms and said something vague. She loved her best friend, but sometimes Anitra just didn't get Sola's situation. For girls like Anitra, there was no pressure to find someone to marry as quickly as possible. For girls like Sola, not so much. Unlike Anitra, Sola was a Dream Act student, and as life-changing as that program had been for her, it wasn't a direct path to citizenship. Scott had been her single best chance to gain legal status until his behavior became so intolerable, she just couldn't see a future with him.

Of course Sola wasn't a complete snake. She really had thought she loved Scott, and had hoped to spend the rest of her life with him. Becoming a legal citizen was only a perk of what she imagined would be a wonderful future as his wife. But then the hair episode had gone down and she'd been so happy not seeing him last semester. Eventually, she'd come to see the writing on the wall as far as their relationship was concerned…and she just couldn't bring herself to use someone she disliked more and more each day for citizenship. So she felt she was doing what was best for both of them when she tried to break up with him.

But that was when Scott, the perfect All-American football player, had shown her his true colors. And Sola might be undocumented, but she knew she deserved better than that. Better than Scott. Better than her captor, who was obviously only looking for someone to replace the

Her Russian Brute

hookers who could no longer drive up to the house thanks to the snow.

Yet here she was, waking up happy and relaxed after a night spent fingering herself over a guy who, wolf punch notwithstanding, had made it clear he was a total dick from the moment she'd first met him, at the door *of a cell he was keeping her mentor and friend locked up in.*

So why was she thinking about him that morning in bed? And later, when she took a shower? Wondering what it would be like to have him, instead of her hand, between her legs. Wondering what it would be like to run her palms over his chiseled body as she rode him—

Seriously, what is wrong with me?! she asked herself, cranking the shower spray nozzle to the right to cool the water temperature.

First order of business—a cold shower to clear her mind of sex she shouldn't be wanting with Ivan, even if he had punched out a wolf for her. And then breakfast.

The shower was easy. Breakfast, not so much. It was the week leading up to Christmas, and Gregory and Hannah had requested the entire week off, wanting to spend the holidays with their grown children and grandkids in town. Sola completely understood why the couple would prefer to spend the holidays with their extended family rather than their grumpy Russian employer and the woman he'd taken prisoner.

But it meant she was on her own for breakfast. This wouldn't have been so bad, except it also meant she actually had to leave her room after avoiding Ivan and her body's reaction to him for six days straight.

It was just a peck on the cheek, she'd been reminding herself since the night of the wolf attack…but her body clearly hadn't gotten the message. She felt a zap of sexual energy go through her at only one touch from him, and she'd been waking up feeling sore and happy ever since.

Sola crept down the back stairs and inwardly cheered as she dashed past the entryway with the Ivan-free armchair under the front stairs. She rushed into the kitchen, seriously hoping he'd stay wherever he was hiding until she finished making breakfast. Something simple and super American, since she doubted Hannah had so much as a black bean in her pantry—

She stopped short, just inside the kitchen door, when she found Ivan inside said pantry, rooting around it, like a bear going after honey.

Her Russian Brute

"Do not run away, I need you," he called out, when she started to quietly back toward the door.

She stopped short again. "Oh, I wasn't running away, exactly," she lied.

Ivan only narrowed his eyes at her over his shoulder, making it clear he didn't believe her.

"You will stop avoiding me now and help me find the cinnamon."

Curiosity brought her further into the kitchen in spite of herself.

"Well, most people would put cinnamon on a spice rack, not in the pantry…"

She walked over to the large Viking stove and pulled down a big container of cinnamon from the collection of spices nestled in the heat-proof rack above the stove.

"What do you need cinnamon for anyway?"

"To make breakfast. I found a recipe on that box for caramel apple pancakes," he said, indicating a collection of ingredients he'd placed next to a box of Bisquick on the butcher block island.

"Yum! That sounds good," she said, her stomach all but standing up and cheering as she walked to the island to set down the cinnamon.

144

But then she took a good look at the ingredients he'd already gathered and frowned. "The recipe called for vanilla ice cream?"

"Yes, it said vanilla."

She picked up the box and chuckled. "Um, actually it just asks for plain old vanilla."

"Yes, plain vanilla ice cream," he said, coming to stand next to her at the counter. "I have everything I need now."

She raised an eyebrow, looking up at him. "So…how many times have you actually cooked before?"

He frowned down at her and grabbed the box. "Never. But how hard can it be?"

See, he is SO arrogant, she pointed out to her body, mentally reminding it why she should in no way be attracted to this guy.

But then he ducked his head and looked at her with an almost shy smile. "Also, after this week we have had together, I would like to cook for you."

F-word. Her sex was basically screaming at her to jump his bones already. Just for saying he wanted to cook for her because she'd had a bad week.

Ugh! Stockholm Syndrome much? she wondered.

Her Russian Brute

Sola took the Bisquick box from him, and muttered, "Thanks, but as curious as I am about how vanilla ice cream pancakes would taste, I think it's best if I take over from here."

Which was how she ended up passing the next half hour under Ivan's watchful gaze as she threw together a batch of caramel apple pancakes.

"You are right. This cooking is not as easy as I thought it would be," he admitted when she set a stack of pancakes in front of him at the kitchen table before sitting across from him with a plate of her own.

"Well, no, it wouldn't be if you've never, ever cooked before. How did that happen, exactly? Did your mom never let you into the kitchen? Or maybe you had servants?"

"Servants. And when I moved out to start fighting, I had people to take care of that for me. I've never had to cook for myself," he admitted before putting the first forkful of pancakes in his mouth.

"So you're a fighter?" she asked, curious despite her resolve to keep her distance. That would explain how he'd managed to K.O. the wolf.

He held up a finger and finished chewing before he

146

answered, "Yes, I was a very successful fighter. I became the EFC world champion shortly before the accident."

"EFC? That's like where you kick box instead of regular boxing, right?"

A small smile lifted his lips. "Something like that. I am trained in a variety of martial arts, including jujitsu. But there is kick boxing involved sometimes, yes."

"I've never watched any EFC fights before, but my dad loved boxing when I was a kid. Some of my earliest memories are of him holding me in his lap while he yelled at the TV." A smile of remembrance lifted her own lips as she cut up her own pancakes. "I bet he would have liked watching you fight. Did you and your dad bond over boxing?"

"No." His voice had gone considerably colder. "My father and I did not have that kind of relationship. He wanted me to be a businessman like the rest of the men in our family. He did not understand why I would want to do anything else with my life."

She chuckled. "Yeah, the only nice thing about being an orphan is there was no one there to tell me how crazy I was when I decided to apply for art school."

A long silence. Then: "I am an orphan now, too. My

Her Russian Brute

parents…died."

She looked up from her pancakes then, and found
him staring down at his plate, his posture one of deep
sadness.

So, he knows how it feels to lose family, she thought,
sad they had this one thing in common.

"I'm so sorry about your loss," she said. "As much
as the students at art school complain about their parents,
they're lucky they don't know what it's like to not have
anyone around trying to tell you how to live your life.
That's the sort of thing you don't know you'll miss until
it's gone."

"No…" he agreed.

Quiet descended over the kitchen as they finished
eating their pancakes. At least Ivan finished his pancakes.
She found she didn't quite have the appetite to finish hers.

"I do not like this sadness between us now," he said
when she stood up and took both of their plates over to the
kitchen's triple sink.

"Yeah," she agreed, pushing the remains of her
pancakes into the small middle sink. "Dead parents
definitely don't make good breakfast conversation."

Behind her, she heard him stand up from the table.

148

"We will talk of something else," he decreed in his domineering way.

But she didn't mind his tone so much, because she was more than ready to change the subject.

"Okay, what should we talk about?" she asked as she began washing the dishes.

"Hannah and Gregory will be gone all week," he said.

It was a casual change of topic, but something about it made her nipples pebble in her bra, especially when he came to stand behind her.

What is wrong with me? she wondered for at least the tenth time that morning. Sola felt like an open-ended nerve. Highly sensitized. Her body was going crazy just because he was standing near her, watching her wash their breakfast plates.

"You know what that means, *da*?" he asked her.

"That we're going to have to figure out something to make for lunch and dinner, too?" she answered.

"That we have the house to ourselves all week," he answered. "No more hiding what we are doing during the day."

"What do you mean hide—?" she started to ask.

Her Russian Brute

But then he reached past her and flicked off the water with one sharp turn of his wrist.

"What are you do—" she started to ask again.

And without any warning whatsoever, his arms came around her from behind. One hand slipping down below the waistline of her jeans, while the other turned her to face him. He took slow, sensual possession of her mouth while beginning to finger the part of her that had been aching all morning…

She was so surprised by the intense intimacy of his actions, she actually let the kiss and fingering going on for a few shocked moments before she remembered who she was. Who *he* was.

"What are you doing?!?!" she demanded, shoving him off angrily. "Stop! STOP!"

Chapter 17

What are you doing?!?! Stop! STOP!"

Ivan froze at her command, and his blood curdled as he belatedly realized why she'd always come to him at night. Under the cover of darkness when she couldn't see his face.

"I see," he said, arms dropping to his sides as he took a pronounced step back. "You only want me like that when it is dark and you can't see me."

She swung around, and he was somewhat surprised to find the huge brown eyes behind her glasses wide with indignation, not the disgust he'd been expecting.

"When have I ever wanted you like that?" she demanded.

He narrowed his eyes, wondering if his near-perfect English was failing him. Or if she were joking, asking him this question in order to humiliate him further.

He answered with the most caustic version of the truth. "When? On the night of the full moon, and every night since then. Last night you climbed on top of me and came three times. I was not sure you would ever get enough before returning to your room."

There, that should put her in her place, he thought, hurt warring with shame inside his chest. But once again, he didn't get the reaction he was expecting.

"Oh... My... God..." she said, as if he'd just revealed to her that he was actually from outer space. "*Oh my God.*"

She swayed a little, and Ivan had to fight the instinct to step forward and steady her. To put his hands on her like she was his woman. Instead he stood there, stiffly watching her repeat the three words over and over again, her entire face a study in shock.

"You came to me," he felt compelled to remind her, voice tight with anger and embarrassment. "I did not touch you because of my face, but then *you* came to *me*."

"No, it's not that," she responded, her voice cracking with what sounded like near hysteria.

Then she took a deep breath before saying, "Okay, here's the thing. I sleepwalk. It's been a problem for me all my life, and it gets especially bad when I'm stressed. Usually it only consists of me maybe wandering around the house a bit and doing things like eating whole cartons of ice cream when I'm trying to stay on a diet. I've learned to control it with a drink or two in the evenings. And the thing is, I haven't been able to have my usual nightcap lately because I've been too scared to go out at night after that thing with the wolf and—oh my God. I just can't believe I…"

Ivan watched her take several more deep breaths as if she were trying to snatch her mind back from the edge of panic. She sounded like she was on the verge of hyperventilating as she squeezed out, "I can't believe this. But obviously it's true—I, um—must have come on to you—had sex with you—while I was sleepwalking."

It was an incredulous story. Unbelievable. Impossible for anyone to take seriously.

Anyone, that is, except Ivan. Who believed her immediately. Who realized as soon as the word "sleepwalking" fell out of her mouth, that every word she was telling him was true. Of course she'd been sleepwalking. What other explanation could there be? Why else would she come to him? Why would she allow someone who looked like him to touch her?

"I see," he said quietly. Because now it all made sense. Humiliating, soul-crushing sense.

Her Russian Brute

"Ivan, I'm sorry. I am so, so sorry," he heard her say somewhere far in the distance, though she was still standing there in front of him. "This is so weird. I mean, crazy. I can't believe it. I can't even imagine how you must be feeling. I'm so sorr—"

He left the kitchen before she could finish the sentence. As it turned out, there was something he wanted even less than her disgust: her pity. He couldn't stand seeing pity for him written so clearly on her face, dripping from every apologetic word.

Pity that a monster, like him, would ever think, even for a moment, that a sweet, beautiful girl like her would want him.

Chapter 18

Sola started the morning off feeling great for reasons unknown, only to end it feeling more terrible than she ever had about anything she'd ever done.

She just couldn't get the stricken look on Ivan's face out of her head. It was like her confession hadn't just hurt him, it had somehow cut him to his core. Just thinking about it made her feel guilty, which was crazy because he was the one holding her prisoner here. The one who'd locked up a feeble old man. The one who'd done nothing but sneer at her since she'd arrived.

Sneer. And save her from that wolf. And make her body tingle with just a few looks while she showed him how to make pancakes…

By the time night fell, she still had no idea what to do about the situation. She still couldn't believe she'd actually walked into his room and done things with him. A lot of things, if his words and the extreme tenderness of her sex were any indication.

Scott never left me feeling like that, she couldn't help

Her Russian Brute

but think…

Only to cut herself off with a shake of her head. A drink. That was what she needed. She couldn't risk going into his room again tonight.

So at 8:00 PM, she did what she would have done the last six nights if she hadn't been so scared of another wolf encounter. She pulled on her snow boots and grabbed a sharp poker from the fireplace. Then she headed down the hill to The Thirsty Wolf, on a mission to make sure this never, ever happened again.

However, her mission was abruptly cut short when a burly guy in a brown leather bomber jacket came to meet her at the door as soon as she set foot in the bar.

"Name's Jed Wolfson," he said, opening his jacket. "I'm the town sheriff."

"Hi, nice to meet you, Sheriff Wolfson," Sola answered carefully, wondering why he was suddenly introducing himself after a week of scanning her darkly from his usual table in the corner. She also couldn't help but note he had the same last name as the one on the manor sign at the bottom of the hill.

"Heard you violated the full-moon curfew."

Oh, so *that* was it.

156

Theodora Taylor

"Yeah," she admitted with an apologetic cringe. "I had a lot on my mind and completely forgot about it."

"You forgot about it," Sheriff Jed repeated, his tone flat.

"Yes, and I'm really sorry," she said, keeping her tone contrite under the stern weight of his glare. "I really didn't mean to cause any trouble."

Sheriff Jed glanced down at the poker in Sola's hand. "Yeah, well. The curfew is in place for a reason. I'm thinking it'll be best for all parties involved if you stay at the kingdom house until the snow melts. No more coming down here after five o'clock."

Sola blinked, barely able to believe her ears. "Wait, you're saying I'm, like, grounded? I can't come down here anymore?"

"Not after five o'clock."

After a moment of standing there, stunned, she came back with, "Okay, well, I'm pretty sure what you're doing here isn't even legal. And I need a drink. Like I *really* need a drink. I'm well over twenty-one, so you can't stop me."

Jed looked down at the ground, considering her words. "No, I can't," he finally agreed.

157

Her Russian Brute

"Thank you," Sola said, moving to step around him.

However Sherriff Jed stepped in front of her again. "I can't stop you. But Lorraine has the right to refuse service to anyone she wants. And from what I understand, you gave her quite a scare the other night. She's probably not feeling all that inclined to serve you after you *forgot* about one of our town's most important rules."

"What? She wouldn't refuse me service. Right, Lorraine?" Sola asked, looking past Sheriff Jed's shoulder to the older woman behind the bar.

But Lorraine averted her eyes, taking a sudden interest in scrubbing the bar with a dishrag.

"He's right, Sola," she muttered without looking up. "It's probably best that you stay with your man at the kingdom house. Less trouble for all of us."

"He's not my man," Sola shot back.

"Really?" asked Jed, arching his eyebrow. "That's not what my nose is telling me right now."

What the ...??? Sola looked around the bar helplessly. Was anyone else hearing the words coming out of this guy's mouth? But all the other bar patrons simply stared back at her blankly, as though every word the sheriff said made complete sense.

158

So she turned her attention back to the only person who really mattered in this bar anyway. The one responsible for dispensing alcohol.

"I just need a drink," she practically begged Lorraine. "I'll even pay you for the bottle and take it with me. I just really need something to drink—please, Lorraine."

But Lorraine refused to look up from pretending to wipe the bar down.

Meanwhile the sheriff snickered and said, "Sounds like you might have a bit of a problem there, Miss Sola. Kind that might need a meeting, if you know what I mean."

A cackle went up from everyone in the bar but Lorraine.

"What? No!" Sola started to argue.

But then Lorraine cut her off. "Just come back tomorrow, Sola," she wearily called out from the bar, refusing to look up from her dogged scrubbing. "I'll sell you anything you want before five."

"You best get on out of here before I have to interrupt my down time and issue you a trespassing violation," the Sherriff told her, low and menacing. "You

Her Russian Brute

git on back up that hill and make sure you listen to Hannah and Gregory. That'll keep you safe until the snow melts."

It wasn't a threat exactly, but it sure did feel like one. And she couldn't help but notice everyone in the bar was regarding her with the same cold stare as the sheriff. A distinct shiver ran up her back as a disquieting feeling that there was something fundamentally different between her and the bar patrons—something that went beyond race or country—came over Sola.

But life wasn't fair, she reminded herself. She knew this and she was ill-equipped to deal with these townsfolk and their strange customs after the day she'd just had. So she left without another word.

A new plan formed in her mind as she stormed back up the hill toward the manor. And why did the locals keep referring to it as the "kingdom house," anyway? Sola shook her head. *Whatever.* She'd tear apart the "kingdom house." Search every room until she found the nightcap she so obviously needed.

She only hoped Ivan wasn't in his usual place when she returned. Parked in the foyer's large armchair like a huge Russian statue, and halfway into an expensive bottle of vodka, waiting for her to come home.

Theodora Taylor

But he was nowhere to be seen when she walked through the door. And the foyer was dark, indicating that no one had bothered to turn on any lights since she'd left the house.

Sola flipped them on now, and started opening doors along the long main hallway. Door after door, determined to find a room with a stray bottle of alcohol.

Her plan eventually worked. She found what she was looking for about five doors in. A study with huge, diamond-paned windows that looked out onto the manor's snowy backyard. Inside was a large pine desk with images of wolves carved into each of its ginormous legs. It looked like a family heirloom, something that might have been passed down for decades, if not centuries.

Unfortunately, Ivan was sitting behind it.

Sola froze in the doorway.

And Ivan stared at her for a long, hard moment, before finally asking, "*Da*? What do you want?"

"Nothing," she answered quickly.

"*Nothing*," he repeated with a sneer. "Then why are you here?"

Sola fumbled, and could come up with nothing but the truth. "Well, I was looking for something to drink.

161

Her Russian Brute

Some alcohol. They wouldn't serve me at the bar down the hill, and I don't want a repeat of the last few nights for obvious reasons."

"Yes, for *obvious* reasons," he agreed in a somewhat mocking tone of voice. But then in a seeming reversal of his usual guest-repelling tendencies, he said, "If you do not like vodka, there are other things to drink over there."

Her gaze followed the jut of his chin to a small, pot-bellied cabinet almost hidden in a dark corner of the study. It turned out to be a mini-wet bar. There were several bottles on top of its marbled surface, and most likely a few more hidden in its squat interior below.

"Oh, thank you," she said, rushing over to it like an addict needing a fix.

Relief hit her like a welcome breeze when she saw the assortment of liquor bottles—not just vodka—lining the bar. She grabbed the first one she came to—rum—not her favorite drink but it would do in a pinch, especially if she mixed it with something from the kitchen.

But before she could walk away, Ivan said behind her, "You will drink it here. As my guest."

An inner groan tore through her and Sola seriously had to fight the urge to run out of the room with the bottle.

Theodora Taylor

The last thing she wanted to do was share a drink with Ivan in his study. Not after what she'd done. What they'd done together.

But his voice was as cold as anything she'd ever heard, and she had no doubt he was faster than her—nor did she think she might be able to convince him to let her take the bottle back up to her room. Ivan didn't strike her as the kind of guy who backpedaled on a command once it was issued.

So with shaking hands, Sola grabbed one of the glass tumblers at the edge of the bar and poured two fingers of rum into it. Then she chugged it, doggedly ignoring the way each tug of liquor burned her throat as it went down.

She slammed the glass down on the hard marble surface, filled it back up, and then immediately chugged two more fingers of rum. Done! Mission accomplished, she thought, as she turned towards the door with a mind to get out of there as quickly as possible...only to slam the back of her right shoulder into a wall.

A huge wall. Made mostly of muscle.

"Are you done with your drink, Sola?" the wall asked.

163

Chapter 19

"Are you done with your drink, Sola?"

Sola quickly moved her shoulder away so she was no longer touching the wall o' Ivan. But she could still feel him behind her. So solid and unforgiving, that if not for the smell of vodka and soap wafting off him, she might have thought an actual wall had suddenly sprouted up behind her rather than a man.

"Y-yes," she answered. "I'm just leaving now."

Two large arms extended from the wall behind her, and hands appeared on either side of her body, resting on the top of the cabinet. He still wasn't touching her, but he'd effectively boxed her in with nowhere to go. And she was too scared to turn around.

"Tell me, Sola, do you like chocolate?"

"What?" she asked. Squeaked, really.

"I believe you heard my question the first time."

"Yeah, sure I like chocolate," she admitted. "But why are you asking?"

"I like chocolate, too," he said, his hot breath

fanning her neck. "Ever since I was a small child, I have considered chocolate a treat. So I asked Hannah to buy some bars for me every few weeks and leave them in one of the kitchen cabinets. But lately, I have noticed something. You see, my chocolate has been steadily disappearing ever since you arrived. When I went to have some tonight, I discovered the last bar was gone. Someone ate all my chocolate. Someone who is not me. Was that someone you, Sola?"

She gulped, remembering the chocolate she'd pretty much binge-eaten along with a hastily prepared turkey sandwich.

"I guess," she answered.

"You guess." He let a beat pass. A beat during which she could almost feel his body pulsing behind hers. Even though he still hadn't touched her. "You like this word 'guess,' I am finding, so I will *guess* a few things now. You say the last time you slept walked, you binged on ice cream because you were on a diet. I am *guessing* now—based on my vanished chocolate and your ice cream binges—that you like sweet things. And when you sleep walk, you do not do silly things like clean the house or go for drive in the car, like some stories I have heard. No,

Her Russian Brute

Sola..."

His nose, just the tip, touched the back of her neck, but it might as well have been his entire hand for the chain reaction it set off in her body. A maelstrom of erotic sensation suddenly erupted within her. Swelling her breast, and making every nerve cell beneath her skin tingle with anticipation.

"...I am *guessing* when you sleep walk, you do the things you want to do. The things you deny yourself when you are awake."

Ugh, she'd never thought of it that way before, but scanning through her past episodes, she could now see he was right. There'd been so many diet-destroying nights that she'd finally stopped dieting altogether. And then there were those times when she'd finally sat down to watch TV after a busy week at school only to discover that someone—very likely her sleep walking self—had caught up on all her favorite shows and then erased them from the DVR. Crazy but true.

And though she didn't share any of this out loud, Ivan seemed to read her thoughts, scraping his lips against the back of her neck as he said, "I am big below, I know. Too big for you not to feel the effects of having me inside

166

you next morning…" His Russian accent had become thicker, darker. "When you wake up with sore pussy, what did you think made it this way?"

His voice was so seductively insistent, it felt to Sola like he was dragging the truth out of her.

"I thought I'd touched myself too hard," she confessed breathlessly, fighting the urge to do it again now. To press her fingers into the throbbing place between her legs.

A dark chuckle erupted hot on her neck, as if no other answer could have pleased him more. And then there was no question about his body touching hers. He leaned over her, covering her from behind and settling a very large erection against the small of her back.

Yet his voice remained casual as he asked, "Does this happen to you often, Sola? You wake up with sore pussy, because you have been masturbating in your sleep? Finally letting your body have what it really wants?"

She bit her lip, unable to answer. Her pussy. Her poor pussy. As sore as it had been this morning, it was throbbing with raw need now. A bittersweet ache building up inside her with every rock of his fully clothed body against hers.

"Sometimes," she panted.

"So you like to do this? You like to touch yourself?"

She didn't answer. Couldn't answer. It was too dangerous, she knew.

But her silence only ratcheted up the tension between them.

"I am going to touch you now, Sola," he announced into the back of her neck. "Now that you've had something to drink, I am going to fuck you with my fingers. And so there will be no more misunderstanding between us, I will make the rules for tonight very simple. I will do what I want to your body, and if you don't want me to do this thing, you will tell me to stop. Do you understand?"

Her lips clamped together, not knowing what to say. Not knowing how to respond. Unable to think beyond the large muscled body crowding her and covering her back.

And then it was too late to talk. His hand was at the front of her. Invading the band of her joggers and slipping between her legs.

A few exploratory dips and then… "I see you are already very, very wet, Sola. I *guess* I will keep going."

He was right. She could feel herself slick with need, and becoming slicker by the second as he worked her with his hand.

"No…" she moaned, unable to believe what her body was doing, how it was responding to him.

"Word I look for is 'stop,'" came his response against her neck. Meanwhile, his large hand kept working her sex, stoking that fiery ache.

One of his hands was inside her, and she could sense the other behind her. He'd pulled his hard shaft off her back and was now clasping it, rubbing it, as if preparing for something more.

No, no, they couldn't…

Sola opened her mouth to tell him to stop. Really she did. But when she tried to speak, his hand pressed down on her button, and all that came out was a long moan.

She didn't remember anything. Not one thing that had passed between them during her episodes. But her body seemed to remember everything. And she seemed incapable of making any protest, until he suddenly pulled away. That was when she found herself mewing in distress, because he'd left her sex empty and her back cold.

"Patience, Sola. I am putting on condom," he informed her from another part of the room. He wasn't

Her Russian Brute

laughing, but she could clearly hear wicked amusement in his voice. "Then I'll give you another chance to tell me to stop."

He was a man of his word. Seconds later, he was back behind her. Yanking down her joggers and panties with his hands, and then pushing into her with his...

Sola's whole body went tight, and she found herself gagging with shock. The size of him, the feel of having something that much larger—so much larger than Scott—inside her most intimate space. She whimpered, not knowing what to do, how to feel...

Then his mouth was at her ear: "Tell me to stop, Sola," he said as he began slowly rocking into her. "Tell me to stop."

With each command, his Russian accent became thicker and thicker. "Tell me to stop," he said into her neck, as if he were just as ashamed of his actions as she was of hers. "Do not let me believe again. Tell me I am wrong. Tell me to stop."

But she couldn't. In fact, when she was finally able to form words, they were the very opposite of the ones he'd requested.

"Don't stop," she moaned. "Please keep going."

170

Theodora Taylor

This was so wrong. So wrong. And she knew better. But he was right. She'd been denying her waking self for nearly two weeks now, and this felt like nothing less than chocolate. Like finally giving into what she really wanted, after years of cold pizza sex with Scott.

Plus, she was too close to stop. She could feel something big and all-consuming coming straight at her, like a sex-fueled freight train. And instead of telling him to stop, she reached back, clawing at his thighs as she begged him, "Don't stop. Oh God, don't stop!"

She could feel his muscles working underneath her desperate hand as he drove into her. His thighs were so large, her hand didn't even cover half of it.

But she was only able to enjoy touching him for a short while. As soon as that last "don't stop" fell from her lips, he snatched her hand away and planted it under his much larger one on the cabinet.

The bottles rattled in front of her as he drove into her, hard and relentless. Not stopping. Refusing to stop, until…

She flew apart. Molecules split inside her, and at least six different arias ripped apart her mind at all once.

She'd never come like this. With Scott. With her

171

Her Russian Brute

hand. With a vibrator. Never in her life would she have imagined something this amazing could happen in her own body.

For eons on end, there was nothing except pleasure, wave after wave of hot light washing over her.

And then she heard him behind her, Grunting hard, his large hand moving to the top of her shoulder, bracing her as his strokes switched from grinding to pounding. Pounding faster and faster until he suddenly sank into the back of her pussy with a yell. She felt his cock jerk hard, right before he emptied into the condom.

He sagged against her then in a rather funny way. Leaning into her, but not giving her all his weight. It took Sola a few moments to realize he was hugging her from behind, cradling her with a tenderness she wouldn't have guessed he possessed.

Which was why it gave her such a jolt when he finally spoke. Thick Russian accent gone, words clear and solemn as he informed her with no guessing whatsoever, "I'm going to take you up to my room, and I'm going to fuck you again, Sola. I'm going to keep you there all night and I'm not going to let you out of my bed until I've done everything you've only been dreaming about when you are awake. Tell me to stop. This is your last chance. Tell me to stop."

How? She wondered in a daze. How could her core be throbbing with need again, aching for him again? So soon after reaching the best orgasm of her life? And how could she tell this large man no?

Her lack of response seemed to be enough for him. The next thing she knew, he was swinging her into his arms, and carrying her out of the study, away from the bar, and into the dark promise of a night without any sleep.

Chapter 20

Sola woke the next morning without her glasses…and without any problem recalling what had happened the night before.

In fact her seriously worked over body gave tender protest as she sat up in what turned out to be her captor's very large bed. And though she'd woken up in an unfamiliar room, she easily found her glasses on the nightstand, right where Ivan had put them before angling his head to give her their first waking kiss—at least the first one she hadn't shoved away from in shock.

Yes, she knew for certain what had happened last night, but she still couldn't believe what she'd done with Ivan while fully awake…what she let him do to her…how she'd screamed…oh, God, how she'd *begged* the night before.

No, now in the cold light of morning—no, scratch that. Afternoon. It was *afternoon*. Already.

She groaned again. Thinking of what she'd done. What she'd have to do now to undo what had happened last night.

Tell me to stop, he'd said. Teasing her all night long.

She should have told him stop last night. Today she definitely would.

After a quick shower and change into yet another set of joggers and t-shirt, Sola did something she'd never done before. She went looking for Ivan Rustanov.

It felt a lot like yesterday's liquor search, but this time it only took three doors to find what she was looking for. He wasn't in the swimming pool or in his study. But yes, here he was, in the gym.

He was in a pair of fighting shorts, punching and kicking an oblong red bag with a deftness she'd never seen anyone display outside of fighting films.

The sight of him like this was completely mesmerizing, and for a moment, all she could do was watch the interplay of muscles rolling under his thick arms and broad shoulder blades as he laid into the bag.

A damp heat erupted between her legs as she watched him, warming her core…making her forget for a moment the reason she'd come looking for him in the first place. To tell him last night had been a mistake. One they couldn't ever repeat, because…

Her Russian Brute

Why was that again, exactly? She struggled to remember her reasons as she crooked her head to the side and watched him work.

But just as she was about to settle down into a full-on stare fest, he came to a sudden stop, head whipping around like an animal that had just scented another in its territory.

"Hi," she squeaked. "Sorry for interrupting. I just wanted to—"

"Are you okay?" he demanded, voice low and rough as he closed the distance between them, not stopping until he was towering over her, all muscle and sweat.

"I'm fine," she answered, a little taken aback by his urgent tone. "A little sore, but that's not why I—"

He cut her off with a bout of language so coarse, she could only assume he was cursing in Russian. "I knew I was too rough with you last night," he finally said, in English. "I should have held back. You are so small. I should have controlled myself better."

"No, I'm fine. I promise," she answered, a little weirded out to be reassuring him that the best sex of her life hadn't damaged her…right before she told him why they could never have sex like that again.

176

Ivan didn't look like he believed her. His light blue eyes gave her another worried scan, and she knew how she must appear to him. In fact, she'd been a little taken aback by the girls-gone-wild look she was sporting when she saw herself in the bathroom mirror earlier. Tousled hair, dark circles under her eyes, lips still swollen from his demanding kisses.

That was the last thing she remembered from last night. Falling asleep with him kissing her, still embedded inside her sex, less hard than he'd been before he'd emptied into the fifth condom of the night, but still nowhere close to being soft.

Her cheeks burned with the memory, and her ears rang with all the things he'd said to her. How beautiful she was, how he'd wanted this from the first moment he'd seen her. *"Tell me to stop, Sola,"* over and over again as he came into four more condoms.

Her eyes couldn't help but drift down his chest, covered in sweat from all that punching and kicking, only to rise when she heard him chuckle wickedly.

"Oh, I see…." he said.

He moved forward, and she stepped back, only to find she'd placed herself right up against a nearby wall.

Her Russian Brute

Very deliberately, Ivan put one hand on either side of her head and leaned in, lips hovering above but not quite touching hers as he said, "You come to find me for different reason."

His accent had gone thick again, his voice husky with teasing amusement.

Oh, God, he was bad. So bad. Like the walking, talking personification of the term "bad boy." But having him this close made her body throb. Made her want things she really shouldn't want. Again.

"No," she barely managed to squeeze out, flattening her hands against his chest. "We can't. I mean, we shouldn't. Ever again."

He met her resistance with a hooded look, his crystal blue eyes studying her lazily, even as he said in a hard tone, "Sola, do not play this game with me. You were awake last night. All last night. You let me in, and now you are trying to kick me out? Why?"

"Because last night was a mistake," she admitted. "A mistake I can't repeat."

He continued to study her so intently that Sola felt trapped, not just by his body, but also by his intense blue gaze. "You were not born here, but I can see you are a very American-style girl. You try to follow the rules and deny yourself all the time. Ice cream. Pleasure. Me…"

He cupped a large hand around the back of her neck, stroking the side of her face with his thumb as he asked, "Why is this, Sola? Why do you pretend you do not want me after spending whole night in my bed? You are a surprising woman, but this is not kind of surprise I like. I will not be toyed with, Sola. Not after last night."

"I'm not…" she stopped, finding it hard to breathe, much less form coherent sentences with him so close. "I'm not trying to tease you."

"Then why do you try to make me believe you do not want me?" he asked, his voice low and fierce. "Why do you keep running, even after I have you?"

"Because I want you, but I don't *want* to want you," she admitted, looking up to meet his angry and confused blue gaze. "I shouldn't want a guy like you."

"A guy like me." He seemed to be sampling her words in his mouth and not liking their taste. "What kind of man do you believe me to be, Sola?"

"Dangerous," she answered frankly. "Last night you made me want things, but now, in the light of day…"

"…you can see my face."

Her Russian Brute

"No! Look…I really don't care about your face," she reminded him, voice weary. "But I *do* care about your heart. You're not a nice guy, and I…don't want to be with someone else like that again."

"The last guy you were with—he was not nice guy." An observation, not a question, and against all possibility his voice had become even harder, his eyes even more intense in their demand for answers.

She shifted inside his wall trap, hating how awkward it felt. That he wouldn't let this go, even though he'd already gotten what he wanted from her last night. Total surrender. Wasn't that enough?

"Anyway…" She looked to the side, no longer able to bear the weight of his angry stare. "You told me to tell you when to stop, and I'm telling you now. Stop."

For a moment he said nothing. Just continued to lean over her, silent and still as a marble statue.

"You are right," he said after a long while. "I am dangerous man. Bad man. I put your teacher in cage. And I made you stay here when I should have let you go. For that I am sorry."

Sola's heart stopped. The last thing she'd expected to come out of this conversation was a sincere apology.

"Th-thank you for saying that," she said.

"No, do not thank me, Sola. Tell me to stop again."

She stared at him, not understanding.

"*Tell me to stop*, Sola," he repeated, his voice little more than a gravelly command.

"Stop?" she said tentatively, doing as he asked but feeling terribly confused.

His response came swiftly. A sneered, "*Nyet!*" And in the next moment, his lips crashed down on hers.

It was like being thrown into an emotional tornado. Around and around went her feelings: surprise and wrong and confused and wrong and hot and wrong and sweaty and wrong and hot…sweaty…Ivan. Nothing but Ivan.

Then he began stripping off her clothes as he told her in a rush, "I never promised you a yes for your stop. The time for asking me to stop was before I met you, Sola, and now…now is too late…too late…"

He had her naked in an instant, and he fell to his knees, locking his lips over her pussy. Her sex, so tender this morning, flamed anew with the first touch of his mouth, the lips of her mound tightening as he lapped at her with his tongue.

The first orgasm came quickly and violently, tossing

Her Russian Brute

her over a cliff without a care for anything she'd said before.

"No, I will *not* stop," Ivan informed her as he stood and wiped her essence off his mouth with the back of his hand. "I cannot stop. I am past stopping."

She shook her head, heart constricting at his words—only to be cut off when he lifted her off her feet, spreading her legs wide around his waist as he pinned her to the wall.

"Do not tell me to stop. Do not tell me to stop… "

His voice was little more than a guttural whisper now, desperate and unhinged as his mouth moved over her neck, her bare shoulders, her chin, all the while repeating, "Do not tell me to stop…"

She wanted to push him away. Knew she should try again to explain in a calm voice why this was such a bad idea…and she would have if he hadn't captured her lips again, devouring all her sensible words and thoughts before she could get them out.

"I need inside you," he said, his accent raw and low as he reached down between them and pulled himself out of his fighting shorts.

And instead of protesting as she should have, she

182

opened her legs wider, groaning when he lifted her up and then oh-so-slowly pushed himself into her. Inch by excruciating inch.

"More," she moaned into his lips. "Need more."

"I do not want to hurt you, Sola," he answered, as he continued to gradually ease himself in. "As much as I want inside of you, I will not hurt you."

But he was hurting her. Her body ached for him now. Ached so bad, his care felt like the worst, most painful teasing. But then, finally, he was all the way inside. Their eyes locked, and he once again brought his large hand up, this time placing it alongside of her face, his thumb wiping away tears she didn't know had fallen from her eyes.

Because she wanted him. Because she didn't want him to stop. Because she couldn't make herself stop.

He took her against the wall, his strokes slow and demanding, as the scent of their combined sexes filled the room. He took his time with her, making her slicker and slicker, using her desire to go in deeper and deeper.

"I do not want to hurt you," he said again. It was more a declaration than an explanation. "All I have wanted to do is hurt people for so long, but not you, Sola, not

Her Russian Brute

you…"

He'd somehow taken full command of not just her body, but her mind. How else to explain what happened next? The way she exploded into stars, glowing with the most romantic opera music as her body milked and milked Ivan's dick.

How else to explain the fierce tug on her heart when he whispered into her afterglow, "No, Sola, I will not stop. I do not ever want to stop. I cannot…I cannot…"

He cut himself off, his body going tight as he flooded into her.

How else to explain their failure to realize he wasn't wearing a condom, until her pussy was drenched with the flood he'd released in her.

"I'm on the pill," she whispered when they were back in his bed. Lying side by side, both exhausted and dazed by what had taken place downstairs. "But the hookers…"

"Girls my cousins sent here. I never touched them," he answered before she could continue. "I have not touched a woman in years. I am clean."

"Why would your cousins send you hookers?" she asked.

184

"Because before the accident, this is what I would have wanted. The fight or the fuck. And I cannot fight anymore…"

"Because it would be too dangerous with your face?"

"Because if I started punching another man, I would not stop. I no longer have it in me to fight only for fun and money as I used to. It would be too dangerous for others if I went back. Even my cousin Boris believes this."

Sola swallowed, processing what he'd just told her. Knowing she should leave it at that, but having to ask, "And your face? Do you mind telling me how it happened?"

There was a long moment of silence. So long, she thought maybe he'd fallen asleep.

But then he told her a story…one that filled her heart with sadness. The story of a spoiled fighter who cared nothing for anyone but himself…until his parents and sister died in a car bombing. One he'd narrowly escaped. The story of how that fighter became a killer, for reasons even Sola could easily understand.

"When I was killing, I felt like I had purpose," he told her in the shadows of his room. "But without the

Her Russian Brute

killing, I only felt dead. I could not abide those girls my cousins sent. Did not touch them, because I was too dead inside. I have not done anything like that since coming here to live. Have not wanted any woman until you showed up like big surprise."

The story of how he became a recluse who lived far from his homeland in the mountains of Idaho, sat between them in the darkening room for a long while after. Sola didn't know how to respond, and Ivan seemed to be done talking.

But then Sola suddenly found herself sharing the story she'd only ever told Brian, Eddie, and Anitra. Everyone else, including Scott, thought her father died of an infection. Which was technically true. But now she told Ivan everything Scott didn't know.

* * *

Ivan lay there in the dark with Sola, not touching her, but listening to the story she told about her life from before.

About how her father had been adrift and depressed after her mother died in an accident at the factory where they both worked in Guatemala. The factory fired him, perhaps in an effort to distance themselves as far from the

186

tragedy as possible, and her father was suddenly out of a job and without legal recourse. He was unable to find work due to his cleft palate. So he packed up his young daughter and took her on a harrowing trip up north. *They fix people like you up there*, he'd been told by friends who knew about such things.

Those friends were right. Her father eventually found an organization that would fund the surgeries needed to fix his palate. And once that was done, he got another job. Not a good job. Washing dishes in the cramped and dingy kitchen of a Chinese restaurant in San Francisco. But as he told his young daughter, this job was much better than the one he'd had back home. Better pay and nicer bosses—plus the opportunity for Sola to grow up happy, educated, and well-fed.

"We shared an apartment half the size of this room with my dad's sister, Ximena, and like fifty million cousins," she joked to Ivan in his gigantic bedroom. "But we were happy."

But then her father's workplace was raided, and three months later, he was deported without his daughter back to Guatemala. He died soon after of a fever, but Sola was convinced it was actually of a broken heart.

Her Russian Brute

He could hear the love she still carried for the man who'd died too soon as she said, "Papa couldn't read or write, but he did manage to call me once before his death. The last thing he ever said to me was 'Be good, Marisol. Be safe. Stay away from those dangerous boys.'"

She explained to Ivan, "I was fourteen. He was scared for me. Any father would be."

And Ivan, who'd never been the least bit curious about the girls he'd slept with before, found himself asking, "How about this aunt he left you with? Did she not take care of you after this?"

"As much as she could," Sola answered. "Aunt Ximena had kids of her own, and even a few grandkids. To her, I was just another mouth to feed. I think she was relieved when I got into ValArts and moved to Southern California."

Sola sighed beside him, her voice tinged with sadness. "I get it. I mean, undocumented life is hard in America, and there were so many of us in that apartment. I just don't think she had it in her to be sentimental about me leaving and never coming back. Still, she did what she could, and I try to send her money whenever I can. I'm allowed to work at the college, even though I'm

188

undocumented, and Brian and Eddie barely charge me rent. When you think about it like that, I'm one of the lucky ones, really."

One of the lucky ones…no "lucky" was not a word Ivan would have chosen to describe her life. "Brian and Eddie? This is the couple you live with? One is old drunk and the other is…sick?"

They weren't touching, but he could sense her stiffen beside him.

"They're more than that," she assured him. "Brian is a brilliant director, and he's been good to be me. He took me under his wing and taught me everything I know about stage direction. And Eddie—he inspires me…"

She went quiet for a long while, before confessing, "I was going to drop out of school, you know. My dad always told me to follow my heart, and I knew from the first time I saw a staged play that my heart was in the performing arts. But it was so hard going to ValArts. All those rich kids, partying and getting high all the time. Being totally okay with taking unpaid internships, because Mommy and Daddy were paying for everything, anyway. At one point, it felt less like I was following my heart, and more like I was being stupid. But then Eddie got sick, and

189

that's when I got it—really got it. I might not be rich or an official U.S. citizen even, but everyone has one thing in common: just this one life to live. And I didn't want to waste mine. Honestly, I don't know how I'm going to make my dreams come true, or even what I'm going to do after I graduate, but I know I have to try. I know my father and Eddie would want me to try. So that's what I'm doing. That's how I'm living."

For moments after she was done with her story, Ivan could only lie there in awe of her. Her resilient spirit and all she had overcome to get to where she was today—only to have a Russian monster come along and ruin it all.

"This is why you do not want to be with me in this way now," he said in the dark, feeling exactly like the scum he was. "You worked very hard to get to your last semester at school and I took away everything you worked for in just one night."

She didn't respond to his comment, but she didn't have to. Her silence was confirmation enough.

He was Ivan Rustanov. Throughout his life, he'd been given anything and everything his heart desired. He'd been offered his first sip of expensive vodka at age 12, his first female companion at age 15, his first super sports car—the original Marussia B1—before he was legally allowed to drive. In his life, nothing had been denied to him, not even revenge for his family's death.

But this small girl humbled him, made him feel for the first time in his life, that he was undeserving, of this life he'd been given, or this angel who'd somehow found her way to where he'd been hiding away from the rest of the world.

"I'll fix what I have broken," he vowed, reaching across the distance that separated them. He pulled her onto her side to face him and once again pushed the curls out of her face. "When the snow melts, I will make this right. I promise you this on my name."

She looked at him, her brown eyes wide with surprise. "Wow, you don't have to do that. I was just telling you my story because you told me yours."

"Sola, understand what I am saying to you now," he said, tipping her face up towards his. "I take care of you now. I have done this thing to your life, and you will let me fix it."

"But—"

He cut her off with a kiss. Not wanting her protests, but needing her mouth.

Her Russian Brute

Besides it was already decided. He might not deserve Sola, but Sola would get everything she deserved.

He would not rest until that happened.

And suddenly, just like that, Ivan's life—which seemed to have hit a dead-end only a few weeks ago—once again had purpose.

Chapter 21

That Sola was going to get exactly what she deserved. Just as soon as he found her.

It was Christmas Eve, and Scott had been waiting outside Sola's house for nearly two weeks. The old man, Brian, had come and gone from the main house a few times, when that nurse came to babysit the crippled fag he lived with. But Sola had yet to return.

Partly out of boredom and partly on a hunch, Scott decided to switch things up that evening and follow the old professor when he left the house shortly after the Mexican nurse's arrival.

Let him have a few, Scott decided when Professor Krantz pulled up to J.J.'s, a strip mall dive bar, and went in. Maybe the liquor would loosen his tongue and he'd be more likely to tell Scott where Sola was when he came out.

But the longer Scott waited for the old man to leave the bar, the angrier he got. It had been almost two hours since the professor had gone in, and it had long since

Her Russian Brute

grown cold and dark inside Scott's Mustang.

Scott's phone lit up, buzzing again with his agent's number.

His new team had unexpectedly made it into the playoffs, and though Scott hadn't been scheduled to officially start playing until the following season, both his agent and his new coach had asked him to bench up for the upcoming games. Scott had agreed to do this back when he thought it would only be a matter of days before Sola returned. The plan had been to wait for her to come home, beg her forgiveness, and then convince her to come back with him to Omaha. Just for the holidays, he'd claim, if that was what it took to get her there.

But she never returned, so Scott had missed yesterday's flight to support his team during the first of their playoff games. A lot of people were mad at him now. And his agent wouldn't stop calling. He'd even threatened to dump Scott as a client in his last voicemail.

All because of Sola.

Yes, he'd beg for her forgiveness. Do whatever it took to get her on the next flight to Omaha with him. But once they got to Nebraska, it would be another story. He'd have to start training her immediately, just like his father trained his mother. He'd have to teach her not to talk back. To be a good wife. The kind of wife Scott deserved.

Scott had a vision of how their life would be together. So clear, it felt like a film in his head. But first he had to find her.

On an impulse, Scott tossed his phone into the car's cup holder, and climbed out. He was sick of waiting.

He found the old man easily. The professor was on the dance floor, dancing to Kid Rock's, *I'm a Cowboy, Baby.* Well, Scott supposed you could call it dancing. The old guy was sloppy drunk and barely able to stand. He was half swaying, half staggering at a completely different tempo to the music. The only thing steady about him was the drink he held tightly in his hand.

Scott scanned the bar. No college kids. Mostly locals, none of which were wearing Suns jerseys or any other sports team gear that he could see. They all seemed far more interested in drowning their individual sorrows than in Scott's arrival.

Good, he thought, making a beeline for the professor. Less chance of anyone rolling tape on the conversation he was about to have.

"Sola send you here to get him?" the guy behind the

bar asked as Scott passed by. "I've been trying to call her for over an hour. Brian is definitely ready to go home."

Scott just nodded at the bartender and laid a hand on Professor Krantz's shoulder. "Okay, Professor Krantz," he started to say.

Brian jerked around and squinted up at him. "Alexei! Is that you?" he slurred, placing one hand on Scott's chest to steady himself. "I've been trying to reach you, man. Sola…you have to call that cousin of yours. Tell him to let her come home."

"What?" Scott asked. Icy anger exploded in him at just the thought of Sola with another man. But of course that's where she was. He'd been too soft with her. He realized that now. He'd wanted their relationship to be a little bit sweeter than the one his parents had. But that had been a mistake. Scott could see that now.

"Where is she?" Scott demanded. "Tell me exactly where she is and who she's with. *Right now.*"

Brian didn't look so much scared by the threat in Scott's voice as confused. "You don't know? But you sent me there, Alexei, you—wait a minute…"

The old man's eyes narrowed on Scott. If not for the situation, which involved him having important information Scott needed, the look on his face would have been comical.

"You're not Alexei! You're that ex-boyfriend of hers. I'm not telling you anything!"

"Now Professor Krantz…" Scott started.

"What are you doing here? Were you following me?"

Scott could almost feel the interested gazes of the few bar patrons land on the two of them. Brian was getting loud, but Scott purposefully kept his voice low as he tried to explain, "I just need to know where Sola is. I need to find her. We had a misunderstanding—"

"I don't like you. I've never liked you," the old man informed him, his face growing redder and more belligerent by the second. "Now get off my property. Before I call the police!"

"This isn't your property!" Scott snapped back at him. "Now tell me where Sola is and who she's with, or I'll—"

The professor once again cut him off. This time with a right hook straight to Scott's face. The punch was sloppy and without much force behind it, but it did the job. Scott's head whipped to the side, and he staggered—more out of

Her Russian Brute

surprise than anything else.

Shouting erupted in the bar, and by the time Scott righted himself, one customer was holding Brian back and the bartender had come from behind the bar carrying a bat.

"Sorry about that," he said to Scott, shaking his head at Professor Krantz. "Brian's obviously had too many. Let's stop this right here. I'll personally make sure he gets home tonight, and he can sleep it off."

"No!" Scott snarled, lunging forward. He was going to kill that old man. Pound him into the ground. *Forget how much Sola cares about him*, he thought—

Scott stopped himself mid-lunge, an idea suddenly occurring to him. An idea that would definitely bring his missing girlfriend out of hiding.

At the very last minute, he backed away, raising his hands in a pantomime of surrender. But it wasn't surrender really. More like the beginning of a new play.

"No," he repeated to the bartender. But this time he added, "*Call the police.*"

Then he smiled calmly at Professor Krantz, the man who would serve as his unwitting ticket to getting Sola back, and declared, "I'm pressing charges."

198

Chapter 22

"Do it, Sola…" Ivan said, his voice low and threatening.

"No, I can't," she answered, shaking her head. Seated as she was—completely naked in his big bed—it was hard, vulnerable work to stand up to him. But Sola couldn't do what he was telling her to do. She just couldn't!

"Sola, this is not a request," the huge, naked Russian sitting across from her said.

"But—" she started.

"No, buts," he all but growled at her. "Now stop making me wait and open your present!"

Sola fingered the box in her hands. It was neatly wrapped with shiny green paper. And she wanted to open it, she did. But she felt too guilty.

"I didn't know we were going to exchange Christmas presents," she told him. "At least not real ones. I was just planning on giving you, like, a really nice blowjob or something."

Her Russian Brute

He grinned at her. "You have already given me a really nice blowjob."

"What? When?!" Sola demanded.

He waggled his eyebrows.

And she let out an embarrassed groan. "Oh, my gosh..." she said with an embarrassed groan. "Did I seriously blow you while I was sleep walking?"

"*Da*," he answered with a lazy smirk. "You also cursed like sailor and complimented me many times on how well I fucked. Would you like me to tell you what else you did while I wait for you to open my present?"

"No..." Sola mumbled, and she began ripping open the gift, if only to distract Ivan from the current topic.

As many things as they'd done together during the days leading up to Christmas, as many stories as they'd shared, she still couldn't get over the fact that they'd had a longer—and apparently more varied—sexual relationship while she'd been asleep.

But all her embarrassment was replaced with sheer glee when she opened the box to find...

"Wool socks! Oh my gosh, Ivan!"

She threw herself across the bed and hugged him before settling back to pull on the thick socks.

"How did you know I needed these?"

She got her answer in another smug smile. "I swear I'm *never* going to go to sleep without at least one drink again."

Ivan just chuckled, low and deep. "Sola, it does not matter if you are awake or asleep. However you want me, you can have me."

She looked up at him, unable to imagine not wanting him, even against her better instincts. But then her smile faded when she remembered their uneven gift exchange. "I only wish I'd gotten you something. This was so thoughtful."

The mirth in his eyes faded as well, and his voice took on a more serious tone as he said, "If you're serious about giving me a gift, there is one thing I would very much like from you."

"Sure," she said, shifting to her hands and knees, mouth already watering in anticipation of his request. "Anything you want…"

But then he said, "I would like the name of the man who hurt you. The not nice guy who bruised your face before you came here to me. This is the only gift I want from you."

Her Russian Brute

Sola sighed, sitting back on her knees. "Anything but that."

"Why not?" Ivan asked. "Are you still in love with him?"

"No!" she quickly assured him with a sad sigh. "I'm not sure I ever *was* in love with him. He sort of swooped in, and I went along for the ride because he was the kind of guy a girl like me is supposed to like. Nice. All-American boy from Nebraska. But then he started becoming more and more controlling, and I knew we had to break-up. That's what I was trying to do when he—when he hit me."

The last four words drew an animalistic sound out of Ivan, and his fists bunched at his sides.

"See, that's why I can't tell you his name. I know what you'll do to him." Not just beat him, she suspected in her heart of hearts. Far worse.

"What I don't understand is why you wouldn't want me to punish this boy for what he did to you. And I know he is boy because a man would never do this to someone he loves."

"You're right, he is a boy," Sola admitted. "That's why I'm with you right now and not him. That thing with him is over."

202

Theodora Taylor

"It's not over," he insisted, covering her hand with his. "Not until—"

"What do you want to do, Ivan? Hurt him? Beat him? Worse?"

Something ticked in Ivan's jaw, and Sola knew, even before he could answer, that "worse" was at the top of his list.

"And then what?" she asked. "Then you come back here and wait for another sad story girl to come along so you can avenge everyone who's wronged her, too?"

He shook his head. "You are more than a sad story girl to me. You know this."

But she shook her head at him. "I didn't tell you that story the other night so you'd feel sorry for me. I don't want your pity, Ivan." She didn't realize how true those words were until she said them out loud.

"I don't pity you, Sola," he said after a long, tense moment.

"Good, then prove it. Leave that other guy out of this. He's something I left behind, and I don't want him here with us. Do you understand?"

She watched his mouth work as he contemplated her request. And she realized in that moment, how different he

203

Her Russian Brute

was from Scott. How unfair it had been of her to dismiss him as nothing more than a spoiled brat that day in the solarium.

Scott had continuously whined throughout their relationship. About his team. About L.A. About all the things that were wrong with the world, as if he was owed everything in this life just because he could run fast and a catch a ball.

But Ivan's sense of right and wrong seemed to go deeper than that, and she could see in the way he struggled with her request that unlike Scott, he truly did care about someone other than himself.

"C'mon..." she wheedled, "My original Christmas gift idea will be so much more fun."

He regarded her for a long, scowling second before leaning back against the bed's headboard and spreading his legs to give her a front row view of the erection nestled between them.

He was hard again, she realized with an inner smile. For her. Not because he pitied her, but because he wanted her, even when she talked back to him. He had no idea how unlike Scott he was in every way.

Or maybe he did. The smile on his face was 110%

204

smug as he gave in with a, "Fine, Sola. I will take this other gift. I admit I am curious about who has more brains: Sola when she is sleeping, or Sola when she is awake."

"Brains…?" Sola's nose crinkled. "Do you mean who's better at giving head?"

He frowned. "Yes, more brains. This is not a slang word you use?"

"Not unless you're a rapper."

"Ah, that would explain it. In my old life, I listened to much rap. I like it much, much better than opera—"

"Ivan?" she interrupted, crouching over his heavily veined erection.

"Yes, Sola?"

"I'm about to get very smart on your dick. Why don't you stop talking while you're ahead?"

* * *

Da, his Sola was smart, *so very smart*, Ivan thought to himself as he stroked her hair. He watched the curly-haired angel between his legs go up and down on his dick with hooded eyes.

It was funny, because before his accident, he'd had more models and actresses go down on him than he could count. But they all paled in comparison to Sola. He'd never met anyone like her before. So innocent and sweet, yet willing to stand up for the people she loved. Full of surprises. And the way she looked at him. He'd lost track of how many times their eyes had locked while they were making love.

Even when it came time for her to leave him in the spring, he knew he'd never forget the way she held his gaze unflinchingly as he moved inside her. She didn't just make him feel like his old self again, she made him feel even better.

She's making me a better man, he thought to himself with another tender caress of her soft curls. His dick pulsed harder inside her sweet mouth. And *da*, she gave even better head when she was awake.

Her coming to his room that night of the full moon had been a very erotic surprise. A life-changing one. But this was even better. He liked being able to watch her in the daylight. Treasured every sound as she wetly sucked his dick, slurping up the pre-cum as soon as it pearled at the head.

Such a pretty picture, but unlike the other girls he'd been with, he didn't feel like he was watching a show. She was sucking his dick because she liked it and because she wanted to make him happy, not because she wanted him to look at her or give her things.

And ironically, that made him want to give her even more. Not only her education—which he owed her anyway. But things like jewelry, clothes…his heart.

Except she already had that, he realized, as a rising sensation started up his spine.

He was crazy about her. Literally and figuratively. He more than liked her already, and it made him feel slightly unhinged. Like no matter how much he did for her, it would never be enough.

For the first time in his entire life, a certain notion occurred to him. He wasn't good enough. He'd been good at fighting. He'd been more than adept at killing. But he was nowhere near good enough for this woman.

A pleasant piercing sensation interrupted his thoughts, and soon after, his dick swelled even larger and a deep growl tore from him as he began to spill into her warm mouth. He came, and came, and came some more, emptying rope after rope of his seed into her throat.

"Good?" she asked, when she was finally done swallowing.

He watched her tongue snake out to catch a drop of

Her Russian Brute

his semen, glistening at the corner of her full mouth, and instantly hardened again.

Seeing his new erection, Sola's eyes widened. "Oh, no, I can't. You've got to give me at least a minute to recover," she groaned with a laugh. Then she rushed to snuggle up against his side as if she were running away from the jutting erection between his legs.

"Take your time," he answered. "It will still be here when you are ready, Sola."

She responded with more sweet laughter, and he relished the sound. Had he ever had a better Christmas? A better moment? Being with Sola like this was better than all his fight wins put together.

"I want to do something more for you," he said, kissing the top of her curly head.

She just laughed and wiggled her be-socked feet against his legs. "I mean these socks are everything. Totally worth the blowjob. Maybe even four more." She kissed his ruined cheek, as always not seeming to distinguish it from the better half of his face. "Seriously, babe, what could be better than this?"

She got the answer to that question about two hours later. After she'd had enough time to recover from Ivan's

208

thank you for his Christmas blowjob, then recover yet again when she'd made the mistake of accidentally pushing her butt into his crotch as they settled in for a nap.

He hadn't been able to leave her alone long enough to sleep much over the past few days. Consequently, Sola was still yawning and a little bleary eyed as he led her through the door of the first room they'd made love in—at least while she'd been awake.

He escorted her to one of the guest chairs, all but setting her down into it, before he went around to the other side of the desk.

"What's this all about?" she asked as she watched him drop into his desk chair with a sleepy smile.

She looked so well-fucked right now, it made him want to carry her back up the stairs and make sure that look never left her face.

But first the gift, then he'd spend the rest of Christmas fucking her, with nothing weighing on his conscience.

"There is no cell phone reception in this town, but the landlines work just fine." He pushed the old-fashioned rotary phone on his desk toward her, and answered her question with a, "Call your professor. Wish him a Merry

Her Russian Brute

Christmas."

"Okay, Brian's Jewish, and doesn't really celebrate Christmas now that Eddie's sick, but who cares? Thank you! Thank you!" she cried.

The look on her face was "thank you" enough. And he knew how important this man must be to her when instead of running upstairs to get her phone, she began the long process of dialing the professor's number on the rotary phone, because she knew it by heart.

"This is amazing," she said when she finished dialing. "He'll be so relieved when he finds out I'm okay." She threw him a saucy smile. "Actually, better than okay."

But then she broke off with a frown. "That's weird. It went straight to voicemail…"

She hesitated, then peeped up at him, biting her lip. "Do you mind if I make another call? Brian might be indisposed, but if I could talk with Eddie's home aide…"

Ivan thought darkly of the man he'd found stumbling around his property and could only bet what Sola meant by "indisposed." He had a bad feeling about this.

But she was looking at him across his desk now, with so much hope and very little guile. He gave in with a, "Yes, of course. One more call. Go get your phone."

210

She shot out of the room so fast, you would think he would have felt better about the decision he'd just reluctantly made.

But instead, he felt worse. Even though he was being the better man for Sola, he had a gnawing worry in his gut. And it only became stronger when Sola returned to the room with her phone and dialed a second number with shaky hands.

She gave Ivan a small smile when she was done. "It's ringing…" she let him know, before breaking off to say, "Hey Vanessa, it's Sola! I tried to call Brian, but his phone went straight to voicemail—"

She broke off, sitting up in her chair with a truly alarmed look on her face. "What do you mean he's in jail? But how…?" Then her face crumpled and she said, "No, Vanessa, I can't. I'm-I'm stuck up here in Idaho. I won't be able to come back until the snow melts. Possibly not until spring…"

The rest of their conversation was drowned out by the ringing in his ears. The same as when that car bomb detonated with his sister and parents inside. Because Ivan knew then…knew, like only a man who'd lost his entire family in one second could know, he'd unwittingly

Her Russian Brute

destroyed what he and Sola had between them.

The dream was over. And real life had just reared its ugly head.

Chapter 23

San Francisco

There were very few things in life that Alexei Rustanov could say he knew for sure. After all, how could a man who'd started out as the scion of a Russian mafia family, only to end up one of the youngest and richest oligarchs in the world, be 100% sure of anything?

But in that moment, on this particular Christmas Day, he knew one thing for sure. He did not like his sister-in-law.

Alexei stood with his fellow losers in the living room of his brother's Georgian mansion. Glaring at his sister-in-law as she waved his baby niece in the air and crowed over Boris's victory as if it were her own. A nicer man would have appreciated how far his tortured younger brother had come with this woman's love. A nicer man would have been happy for Boris, who now held up the trophy that had been Alexei's until five minutes ago.

But Alexei was not a nice man, and he was already

Her Russian Brute

plotting his brother's downfall in the next round of diaper changing dominance—

Chirp! Chirp! Chirp!.... Chirp! Chirp! Chirp!

His scheming thoughts were interrupted by the electronic chirping of the phone in his pocket. He pulled it out, and smiled when he saw the name on the screen.

"It's Ivan," he announced, and a hush fell over the formerly noisy room.

Because Ivan—the young cousin who'd become a recluse after his horrible accident and made a habit of not returning his calls—was calling Alexei on Christmas. It seemed to Alexei, and probably to everyone else in the room, like nothing less than a Christmas miracle.

A sentimental string tugged at his heart as he answered the phone, preparing to say, "*Schastlivogo Rozhdestva*"–Russian for "Merry Christmas."

However, Ivan started talking in a blur of Russian before Alexei could so much as get the first syllable out.

Of course he responded to his young cousin's requests as best he could. But by the time they got off the phone, Alexei was even more agitated than he'd been when he'd merely been plotting the takedown of his brother and sister-in-law.

214

But family was family…

He turned to Suro, the head of his American security force, a man who'd become one of his most trusted friends over the years, and said, "Ivan needs a helicopter sent to his home in Idaho."

"That can easily be arranged," Suro assured him with a small bow.

"Is he coming here?" Boris asked, hope lighting his normally stern face.

"No, I don't think so," Alexei answered, not bothering to keep the bafflement out of his tone. "He wants it for…a girl."

The whole room went silent with shock. The Ivan Boris and Alexei had known before the accident had been so spoiled and pampered, he wouldn't have lifted a finger to help a woman out of a car, much less with something as big as what he'd described to Alexei on the phone. And the Ivan they all knew now was more likely to callously insult a woman than go through such great lengths to help her.

Which was why it felt like his sister-in-law was speaking for the entire room of when she said, "Girl? What girl?!?!"

Chapter 24

Brian may have had difficulty contacting Alexei Rustanov. But Ivan not only got in touch with his cousin as soon as she updated him about Brian, he also convinced Alexei to send them a ride out of Wolfson Point.

The only thing Sola found harder to believe than the sight of the black machine touching down in Ivan's backyard, was that he was coming with her.

"You don't have to do this!" she said after they'd settled in their seats and put on the special noise-cancelling headphones that allowed them to still hear each other over the *thwump! thwump! thwump!* of the helicopter blades. "I've always taken care of things with Brian. I can handle this myself."

He sneered. "I told you, Sola. I take care of you now," he answered over the headphone's private line. "I will not leave your care to a drunk who is now in jail."

Harsh, but Sola was too grateful for the helicopter to fight him on this. A few minutes later, she was ascending into the air on her first ever helicopter ride. The last thing she saw of the strange mountain town she'd been living in for two weeks were several Wolfson Point residents—many of them still in their Christmas pajamas—spilling out of their houses to see what was causing all the racket.

A few of them waved, and she waved back, not knowing how to feel about the town she was leaving behind. Or if she'd ever see it again.

The feel of a large hand squeezing around hers brought her out of her thoughts.

"Thank you," she said to the man sitting beside her. "If not for you…"

"You would not have been trapped here in the first place," he finished, his tone flat and angry. "Do not thank me for this, Sola. Do not thank me for any of it."

This was no longer the Ivan she'd come to know over the past few days. The unexpectedly warm and sensual man was gone, replaced with a cold commander who gave clipped instructions to everyone he encountered. And he didn't seem impressed at all with the fact that they were in a helicopter. A freaking helicopter! Or even with the private jet that met them at a nearby airfield to ferry them back to Van Nuys .

And the limo that picked them up on the tarmac in

Her Russian Brute

California? Nope, not a hint of wow! ever made it onto Ivan's face.

By the time they reached the Santa Clarita Valley Sheriff's Station, the reality of how different Ivan was from her was beginning to settle in. They might have connected on a deep level in Idaho, but out here in California, it felt like their two worlds couldn't be further apart.

A slim lawyer with a great tan and an expensive suit met them at the station doors. In what might well have been the most anti-climatic Brian episode of Sola's life, the lawyer explained to her that he'd already "arranged" for Brian's release, which apparently included getting those pesky assault and disturbing the peace charges dropped, too.

He smiled at her with a mouth full of shiny white teeth as if to say getting art school professors out of bar brawl charges was all in a day's work.

"He'll be out any minute," he assured Sola.

"Thank you," she said, completely stunned by this turn of events and grateful beyond words for the lawyer's work on Brian's behalf.

But Ivan didn't say anything. Just… "And the other

matter?"

The lawyer sobered. "Yes, perhaps we should discuss that outside."

Ignoring the questioning look she was practically drilling into his back, Ivan disappeared through the main doors, speaking a whole bunch of Russian with the lawyer who she assumed was either Russian or bi-lingual.

"Marisol! Marisol!"

She turned at the sound of Brian's voice and ran across the station straight into his open arms.

"Thank goodness you're all right, dear girl!" he said, hugging her tightly and kissing her head. "I was so worried about you! How did you get here? Did that Russian brute let you go? Did you escape? And if so, how did you get out of that godforsaken town?"

Sola had to laugh that he seemed way more concerned about her than the fact that he'd just spent a night in jail on assault charges. "Brian, I'm fine. But how are you?"

"None the worse for wear," Brian insisted, smoothing a hand over his very wrinkled clothes. "I think I may have burned a bridged with J.J., however."

"Yeah…" She withdrew from the hug, thinking of

Her Russian Brute

the bartender who'd called her countless times to get Brian with a wince. "I'm pretty sure you're no longer welcome there."

"No, I suppose not," Brian said regretfully. He shook his head. "What a bizarre night. I don't remember any of it, you know, but I'm told I became rather, ah, rough with a young fellow. I tell you, I would've paid good money to see me engaged in fisticuffs! I don't think I've been in a fight since my Vietnam days…"

He chuckled.

But Sola didn't. "Brian. You got in a fight. At a bar. Like an honest to God bar fight. Do you know what could have happened to you if Ivan's lawyer hadn't stepped in?"

"Ivan's lawyer? Brian repeated as if she'd just introduced a totally foreign concept into the conversation. "Do you mean to tell me that Russian brute is the one who arranged to get me out of jail?"

"Yes, that's exactly what I'm saying," Sola answered. "And if he hadn't, you could have been sued, lost your job, had this on your permanent record making it impossible for you to get another job…"

"I know, dearest Marisol, I know," Brian insisted, patting her shoulder and guiding her toward the station

220

doors. "I'm sorry about all of this, I am, but I'm going to be better from now on. I promise."

"That's what you said last year in New Mexico." All those missed morning rehearsals, one of which had been a full dress. Sola's gut churned just thinking about it. And she was graduating this year. Who would take care of Brian then?

"But I mean it *more* this year," Brian insisted with an impish smile. "Trust me, nearly twenty-four hours in the pokey gave me quite a bit of time to think about the error of my ways. But enough about me, dear girl," he said, before Sola could argue with him further. "I want to hear all about how you got that Russian fellow to get me out of my latest debacle. I'm guessing there's quite a story behind this deus ex machina!"

"Well, I wouldn't exactly call it a deus ex machina," she said as they headed for the station doors.

But then they walked out to find Ivan leaning against the passenger door of the limo. Seeming so much bigger and more powerful than any other man she'd ever known. *Not God,* her strict Catholic upbringing reminded her. But definitely god-like.

Brian must have felt it, too. He was

uncharacteristically quiet in the limo. Sitting next to Sola, both hands wrapped around one of her arms. Like a child afraid of his father's rebuke.

Like she was the mentor and he the mentee.

"Sola tells me I have you to thank for all of this," Brian finally got up the courage to say to the glowering hulk of a man sitting across from them in the back of the car. "I really am very sorry for any trouble I've caused."

He looked over at Sola, his face wrinkling with sorrowful confusion. "I don't remember much about last night. Just that I'd had a bad day with Eddie, and I was oh so worried about you, dear Marisol. I thought a drink or two would help calm my nerves…"

"Do not," came Ivan's clipped voice from the other side of the car. "*Do not* put this on Sola, old man. My cousin says he never heard from you. Not one word."

"That's because I didn't know how to reach him. He sent me up to that town to check on you, but when I tried to call his office to ask him to help Sola, his assistant said he was out of town and wouldn't be taking calls for the next two weeks. I didn't know what else to do…"

"So you just gave up?" Ivan asked. "This girl, who considers you a second father, who dropped *everything* to come to your rescue, who gave up her schooling so you might return to your husband...she did *all* of this for you and you repay her by abandoning her? To get drunk in bar and cause her even more trouble by fighting and getting arrested?"

By the time Ivan was done, he was dropping articles and his Russian accent was as thick as Sola had ever heard it. But Brian must have understood every word. For a moment, he wilted under the heat of Ivan's scorn. But then he rallied with, "It wasn't my fault! None of this is my fault." He squeezed Sola's arm. "Surely you understand that, dear girl. I don't even remember what happened last night, exactly!"

"Exactly," Ivan snarled, his tone laced with acid. "That is because you were too drunk to remember. Too drunk to take care of your spouse or Sola properly."

This was getting out of hand, Sola thought. "In all fairness, it's not his job to take care of me," she pointed out to Ivan. "I knew what I was getting into when I accepted that deal with you, and he has Eddie at home—"

But Ivan cut her off. "Sola, do not do this," he said, leaning forward to take her free hand in both of his. His eyes gentled, but his tone was low and fierce as he said, "I

Her Russian Brute

know you care for this man, but he is a drunk hiding behind a young woman. My cousin Alexei had no idea he had drinking problem, but you have not seem surprised by any of this. I think this is because you are a very nice girl who has been covering for this man you love for too long. This cannot go on."

Ivan's words hit her like a ton of bricks, even as she realized their truth. She loved Brian. And she'd been bailing him out for longer than she could remember now, making so many excuses for him that it was hard to see the truth of just how bad he'd gotten until Ivan laid it out in front of her in his stark, Russian way.

As if on cue, the limo came to a stop and Ivan said, "We are here."

Both Sola and Brian's eyes widened when they looked out of the tinted windows and saw where "here" was. Not their Valencia home, but a gated property with a discreet sign bearing the words, New Promises.

Sola wasn't a recovering anything, but she'd seen enough of her fellow art students get whisked away by worried parents after one too many drug binges to know this was a rehab facility.

"No! No!" Brian whimpered beside her.

224

As gentle as his tone had been with Sola, Ivan shot Brian a look cold enough to freeze. "Sola cares about you deeply, and she wants you to remain in her life for reasons I do not quite understand considering all you have put her through. I, however, am not Sola. I am not so blinded by gratitude and loyalty to you that I am willing to see past your faults."

Ivan glared at Brian, his crystal blue eyes hard as ice. "I will not have her hurt. By you or anyone else. So here is my offer. I will make sure your bar fight stays out of the public record. I will pay all your outstanding medical bills. I will hire additional help for Eddie, so the burden of his care is not so much on you. But *only* if you go into this rehabilitation program."

Brian thought about Ivan's offer for a moment, but then shot back with a mutinous frown, "And if I say no?"

Ivan glowered, but before he could respond, Sola turned to her mentor.

"Brian, why would you say no?" she had to ask. "You're drowning in medical bills, and…" She didn't realize the truth of her next words until she said them out loud. "You can't go on like this. You're killing yourself with alcohol, and if you keep it up, the next fight might

Her Russian Brute

end in something far worse than assault charges."

"What could be worse, Marisol?" he suddenly demanded with ugly derision in his voice. "Watching the man you love become increasingly demented and catatonic, day in and day out? Knowing he only has a year at most left, and things will just get progressively worse for him until the end? This is not the life that beautiful man deserves! He's being taken from me, bit by bit, and there's nothing I can do about it. Not one damn thing!"

"Oh, Brian," Sola said, when the older man broke down in helpless tears.

She pulled him into her arms. Rocking him back and forth as he cried for the man he'd expected to share the rest of his life with only to have everything upended by cruel fate. "Life isn't fair. This isn't fair," she said. "But…you have *got* to accept Ivan's offer."

"Marisol, it was just one fight," he sobbed into her shoulder. "I'm not usually that bad, am I?"

Sola loved him. Loved him as much as if he were really her father. And because she loved him, she told him the truth.

"Brian, the only reason Alexei hired you to spy on Ivan, the only reason you still have a job, and the only reason you're still getting hired for summer opera gigs, is because I've been covering for you since Eddie first got sick. I know watching him go through this has been more than upsetting for you. But you've got to be better than this. For him. For me. Most of all, for yourself. You're not the man I respect and love when you're drinking. So please take Ivan's offer. Get better. That's all I want for you."

Brian sniffed. Then he sat up and rubbed a shaking hand over his face. "Oh, dear, I really crapped the bag on this one, didn't I? I'm sorry, Marisol."

"Don't be sorry," she returned, her own eyes filling with unshed tears. "Just go in there and get through this."

She and Brian walked hand and hand to the gate, and she gave him a tight hug before he disappeared into a pretty stucco villa with an intake counselor. "Thank you," she said to Ivan when she returned to the limo.

He didn't answer, just kept staring out the window. All gentleness was gone from his face again, and this time it stayed gone. This should have felt like a happy ending, with Brian tucked safely away in a rehab facility, Sola didn't feel very happy at all as they rolled away from New Promises. In fact, there was something very bleak hanging

Her Russian Brute

in the air between them. Something that made her feel like they'd already lost everything they'd had together over the past week, even though Ivan was sitting across from her.

Chapter 25

The first thing Sola did when she got back to the home she hadn't seen in weeks was check in at the main house.

"Want to come with me to meet Eddie and Vanessa or wait at my place?" she asked, holding out her keys to the hulking man who'd exited the limo with her. She already knew how he'd answer, but wanted to give him a choice…

He glanced at her. Glanced at the little house she'd happily occupied for the last few years.

"Your place," he answered.

Ivan looked tired, his eyes more hooded than usual, his half-burned face drawn. Too much socializing, she guessed. He'd been alone for so long, and now he'd had a lengthy, drama-filled day. And he couldn't even decompress in his own surroundings.

It was on the tip of Sola's tongue to thank him. Yet again. Honestly, she didn't know if she'd ever be able to thank him enough. But he was already on his way to the

Her Russian Brute

guesthouse. Like a cold winter bearing down on the quiet little California cottage. She couldn't help but note that he seemed out of place in her world. Almost as out of place as she'd been in his Idaho manor.

Sola sighed and headed into the main house. Eddie was in the kitchen, sunken down in his wheelchair at the room's round wooden table. When Brian first introduced his new T.A. to his husband, he'd been a big and burly actor with a booming voice. He'd been known for playing thugs in nineties comedies until he aged out. And like most actors who were really good at playing villains, he'd turned out to be kind and warm, welcoming Brian's protégée into their lives with open arms.

But today, he sat bent and painfully thin, mouth partially hanging open. He needed a haircut, Sola noted, scraping the hair out of his eyes, and pressing a kiss to his papery forehead.

"Hi, Eddie," she whispered. He only stared into the distance, his eyes unfocused and dull, which meant he was having a catatonic Christmas day. It was sad but it was also a blessing compared to the days when he would rage from his chair, accusing anyone who came through the kitchen of being ghosts from his past. Men who had hurt

230

him. Women who had said cruel things to him. And vice versa. Sometimes apologizing to her, Brian, and Vanessa with tears in his eyes.

Looking at Eddie now, Sola felt better about pushing Brian to get help. No, he didn't want to be away from his husband. But the three-month break he'd get from his role as a part-time caregiver on top of holding down a full-time job would certainly do him good.

"Merry Christmas, Sola! Did Mr. Brian make it to New Promises okay?" a voice asked behind her.

Sola looked over her shoulder to see Vanessa come in with a basket of laundry. Apparently Ivan had been so sure about Brian accepting his proposal, he'd already had his lawyer explain the situation to her. Vanessa was clearly excited about expanding her hours, and told Sola she had a cousin who was eager to work alongside her as Eddie's assistant aide.

"I'm so sorry you had to take care of Eddie all by yourself on Christmas Day," Sola apologized.

As they'd agreed in the beginning, they spoke only English in Eddie's presence, both deeply aware he was still listening, despite the limitations of his body and brain.

"Oh, it is no problem," Vanessa assured her with a

Her Russian Brute

wave of her hand. "Big bonus your boyfriend give me more than made up for it."

Her boyfriend...

Sola let the word bounce around in her mind. *Boyfriend.* But no, not really. Strange...Ivan felt like so much more than a boyfriend. Her lover. Her savior. Her friend. Her man. Her confessor. So many words to describe his relationship to her, but nothing that completely summed it up.

"I saw him through the window," Vanessa confessed, setting the hamper on the table. "He's big, and maybe you don't mind his face so much, no?"

Sola half smiled, thinking of how many times he'd accused her of not liking him because of his face. "No, I'm fine with his face," she answered.

But his attitude—that still needed some work, she thought as she walked across the back lawn and into her guesthouse for the first time since early December.

Something inside her went a little cold when she found him in the living room. His black pea coat still on, like he was getting ready to leave at any minute.

"I need his name," he said, before Sola could so much as say hello. "I need the name of the man who hit you."

"Why don't you take your coat off?" she asked, coming to stand in front of him.

But when she started to unfasten the large silver buttons, he grabbed both her hands in his. "I need his name, Sola. I can't leave you here, knowing he's still out there."

"Who says you have to leave me here at all?" she asked him, putting a lot of effort into keeping her tone soft and teasing.

"This is no joke."

"I know that," she answered in a more serious tone. "But Ivan…you're talking about leaving already."

He stopped then. Breathed. "Sola, I cannot be here in this place with you. Little houses in small towns are not my way of life. And my face—"

"I don't care about your face," she reminded him.

"You are only one who does not care. Everyone else stares." He shook his head. "I must go soon—I cannot be here."

She let out a sad breath. "Okay, I understand. I've got school, and you've got your life as a recluse to get back to."

233

Her Russian Brute

"Good, you understand," he said. Either not getting or choosing to just plain ignore her dig. "Then you will give me his name, and I will make sure he does not bother you again."

"I also understand we don't have much time left together, and I don't want to waste it."

"It would not be a waste," he insisted, tone harsh as the Idaho mountain he lived on. "Protecting you could never be waste of time, Sola."

"Ivan, please," she said, her heart breaking at the prospect of him leaving. Like what they'd had in Idaho meant nothing to him. Like *she* meant nothing to him.

Sola began unbuttoning his coat with frantic urgency.

"It's been a long day, and I don't want to argue about this anymore. I want you." She kissed him. Once, twice, with all the desperate passion in her heart. "All I want is you. Can it just be you and me again? Just for tonight? And then we'll figure out all that other stuff in the morning?"

Ivan looked away, and she could almost see something ticking in the mottled skin that covered his jaw.

Then, as if making a decision, he took her in his

234

arms and kissed her with what felt like a year's worth of pent up passion. Even though they'd been together only that morning.

But the kiss—and the sex that followed in her relatively tiny bed—felt like a good-bye. And it was all Sola could do to keep from crying as his large body rolled over hers.

Giving her his passion but reserving his heart.

* * *

Sola fell asleep holding on to Ivan tightly, but was surprised to find him still there when she woke the next morning.

She looked down at the large man taking up most of the space in her tiny bed with wonder. He kept his room at the manor the very opposite of hers. Dim and in shadows, so it was nearly impossible to see his face.

But she could see it clearly now in her brightly lit bedroom. One side was mottled and red. The other side…less interesting, but even more beautiful somehow for its contrast with the other.

She pondered, not for the first time, his life before the car bomb that had killed his family and ruined half of what looked like a very handsome face. How many women had there been? Obviously a lot. He knew how to please a woman, and you didn't get those kind of moves without a lot of practice.

Looking down at him, she resisted the urge to touch the smooth side of his face and whisper, "Mine," to any would be takers.

Crazy. Not just because it was too soon to feel so strongly about him, but because he'd pretty much already told her he'd be leaving any minute now.

Breakfast, she decided. That was exactly what this situation needed. Something, anything, to keep him there a little while longer. As much as she'd hated this man two weeks ago. She was nowhere near ready to let him go now.

Of course everything but the cereal in her kitchen would be long expired by now. But shopping for groceries was one of Vanessa's duties, and she always had the staples lying around.

Thinking about the authentic Guatemalan breakfast she could make for Ivan this morning, Sola pulled on a robe and gingerly jogged in her bare feet across the concrete carport driveway that separated her guesthouse from the main house. Sola edged around Brian's Lexus, which Brian had taught her to drive, even though she couldn't technically apply for a license. She shook her head at the car, barely able to imagine going back to her life at ValArts to finish her year after everything that had happened.

"Hey Vanessa!" she called out as she entered through the back of the house and headed toward the kitchen. "I need to borrow some milk and eggs for…"

She stopped in the kitchen doorway when she saw who was seated at the kitchen table across from a catatonic Eddie.

It was Scott.

And Vanessa was sprawled across the kitchen floor behind the table, obviously having been knocked out by the butt of Scott's gun. But he had the point of his gun trained on Eddie.

Until he spotted Sola standing in the doorway. At which point he swung the gun away from Eddie, aiming it directly at her.

"Hey, Sola," he said. Scott's words were friendly enough, but his tone was as sinister as anything she'd ever heard. "I was wondering when you'd join us."

Chapter 26

Scott was no longer attractive to Sola. Not now that she'd been found and thoroughly seduced by Ivan Rustanov.

But he *really* didn't look good this morning. His perpetually clean-shaven square chin had been overtaken by patchy stubble. His clothes were rumpled, and she could smell him all the way from the door.

She was reminded of the version of Ivan she'd first encountered in Idaho. But only a little. Ivan had been like a wounded beast, one who hadn't quite figured out how to start taking care of himself again. But Scott just looked crazed, his brown eyes glittering with obvious madness.

"Scott," she said as calmly as she could. "Put down the gun. Let's talk about this."

"No, I think the time for talking is over, Sola," he answered, knocking over the chair as he stood up. "I wanted to talk three weeks ago. I came back the very next day after our fight to talk to you, to try to make you see reason. But you weren't there. So I waited and waited for you to get back, only to find out you've moved on to some other guy. Who is he? What's his name?"

Suddenly she had that not-quite déjà vu feeling. Another man asking her for a name. But for a completely different reason.

"It doesn't matter," she answered.

He huffed out a bitter laugh. "There you go again, Sola. Talking back..." His face twisted into a condescending sneer. "Of course it matters. I had a plan. Use my charges against that drunk professor of yours to smoke you out, then offer to drop them if you came back to Omaha with me."

So much crazy in three sentences, Sola had to struggle to find her next words.

"That was you? You're the one who pressed charges against Brian for hitting you? But you're so big and he's so small!"

"I did it for you," Scott answered, his voice little more than a thin whine. "I did it to make sure we could be together."

She covered her mouth, struck by what Scott had done and how little remorse he had to show for it. She wanted to punch him for what he'd put Brian through,

Her Russian Brute

making him spend the night in jail.

But he was the one with the gun, and she was the one with everything to lose if he started shooting. Including Eddie and Vanessa.

So she asked him in low, trembling voice, "What do you want, Scott. Whatever you want, I'll do it. Just please put down the gun."

Scott frowned, like her sudden acquiescence was distasteful to him. "What I wanted was for us to be together in Omaha. Husband and wife. What I got was a faithless slut who hopped into another man's bed as soon as I turned my back on her."

"We broke up," she reminded him. "We were over—"

"We're not over until I say we're over!" he screamed at her.

He broke off, seeming to put immense effort into calming himself. And when he spoke again, he once again sounded like the oh-shucks farm boy she'd thought he was when they first started dating. "But that's alright, Sola. This too shall pass, and I'm glad I'm finding out about your slut proclivities now. We can get past this. I'll train you…after you come home with me."

240

The thought of going anywhere with this lunatic curdled her stomach, but she grabbed on to his demand like a lifeline.

"Okay, fine, I'll come with you. Anywhere you want to go. Let's get out of here. Right now."

Saying the words felt like the worse betrayal. Of her values, of the man lying in her bed, but the thought of Eddie or Vanessa getting hurt by Scott scared her way more than anything else.

"You'll have to pack a bag, and that…" Scott face once again screwed up into a disgusted grimace. "…that *other man* is still at your house."

"No, I don't need to take anything with me," she assured him quickly. "And I've got my phone. I'll call him," Sola offered, pulling her phone out of the pocket of her robe and waving it like a white flag at Scott.

"Do it," Scott said. "Call him off, and we'll talk about letting you and your friends live."

Sola punched in the number to the landline at her guesthouse. Thank goodness Brian had never gotten around to taking the old phone line out, even though she never used it.

"*Da*, hello…" a gruff, sleep-worn voice answered

Her Russian Brute

after a few rings.

"Hi, it's Sola," she said, doing everything in her power to keep her voice from shaking. "I hate to do this to you, but I decided to go visit my family in San Francisco for a few days."

A pause, then came a very flat, "You continue to be full of surprises, Sola. Why would you do that?"

"Because this obviously isn't going to work out between us," she answered. "And I'd rather just rip off the Band-Aid now and save us both a lot of pain later. Thank you for everything, but when I get back, I'm thinking you shouldn't be here."

Another long pause, then, "Fine, Sola." And he hung up.

Her heart clenched at the thought of him ending the call so coldly. It was what she wanted. What would keep him safe, but still...

She blinked the tears out of her eyes and turned to Scott. "I did it," she told him, holding back a small sniff.

Scott weighed her words, lowering the gun a little as he did so. Then he said, "Okay, let's go. We'll take the fag's car so you can drive." He indicated why it was necessary for her to drive with a shake of his gun.

242

"We'll get you something to wear on the way to the airport. Just don't try anything funny, Sola," he warned. "If you do, I'll come back here and kill Eddie and that nurse, and anyone else who gets in my way."

Sola nodded quickly. "I get it. Just please, let's go."

Quickly, she added to herself, *before Ivan's car gets here to pick him up.*

The last thing she wanted was for Ivan to get caught up in any of this. And she let out a sigh of relief when Scott pointed his gun toward the back door, indicating she should go out first.

Sola walked towards the door, happy to get Scott away from Eddie and Vanessa. Only to suddenly hear Scott yell behind her, "No, get back! Stay away!"

She stopped short and that's when she saw someone coming through the back door.

"No!" she screamed, knowing who it was, even before she could see him. Scott would kill Ivan, she knew. Kill him without blinking, and think it was totally within his rights to do so. Without thinking, she turned and sped toward Scott, who already had his gun raised.

She pushed him back into the kitchen, taking him by surprise. He dropped the gun and stumbled backwards.

243

Her Russian Brute

The weapon skittered across the floor and Sola dived for it, desperate to get to it before Scott could.

But just before she could hook it with her fingers, a hand grabbed on to the back of her jeans. Scott pulled her back with all his football player muscle and flung her against the kitchen wall like a ragdoll before going after the fallen gun.

However, just as Scott grabbed the gun, something large rushed passed her.

"What the—!" Scott yelled, raising his gun to shoot.

Ivan moved so fast. His hand was around Scott's neck and the gun was clattering to the floor again before the two words were even fully out of the football player's mouth.

"Ivan!" Sola gasped, pushing herself off the wall.

Scott's breath cut off with an ugly hitch. "Sola!" he choked out, trying to appeal to her for help.

"No, do not talk to her. Do not even look at her." Ivan squeezed Scott's throat harder. "You do not get to have her in these last moments. My voice will be last you hear. My face the last you see."

Ivan was right about that. A few moments later, Scott fell to the floor beside Vanessa, his windpipe

244

crushed and his life ended under the force of Ivan's one-handed chokehold.

Ivan came to stand over the fallen football player. Breathing hard, and looking like he wanted nothing more than to pick up the gun Scott had dropped and kill the dead man some more.

"Ivan," Sola whispered.

He looked at her, eyes intense. This was the killer she'd been afraid of unleashing, Sola realized, staring at him wide-eyed. But now that killer had just saved her life.

"You see the real me now," Ivan said. "You understand what lies beneath."

"No, no," she assured him. "I only see the man who just saved my life and their lives too." She gestured at Eddie and the still prone Vanessa. "Please don't think I'm judging you at all now."

She reached up to touch him, but he grabbed her hand before she could. "You are too kind, Sola. So kind, you are surrounded by broken people who take advantage of you."

"No," she answered, hating that he saw her like that.

But Ivan shook his head, insisting. "I am not the man you deserve."

Her Russian Brute

"Well, I wouldn't say that!" another voice suddenly said. "I wouldn't say that at all."

They both turned, startled to see an alert Eddie at the kitchen table, his face lit up, his eyes vibrant again despite his body's sunken demeanor.

"I never did like that boy, Marisol," he informed Sola. And to Ivan he said. "But you—tall, blonde, and scarred—seem like a keeper. Russian, right?"

"*Da*...yes," Ivan replied, squinting at him. "And you are Eddie. Sola has told me much about you."

"Did she tell you I performed in a play in Russia once?"

An awkward beat. "No," Ivan confessed. "She did not tell me this."

"Chekov. A dazzling production. I ended up fucking the director after the run was done. He had a rather large dick. I'm thinking you might, too. Am I right?"

Ivan looked over at Sola, obviously not knowing how to respond. "So this is the dementia stage of his illness?" he asked her.

"No, actually, this is Eddie," Sola answered, stepping forward with a huge smile. "The real Eddie. He's always like this."

246

She bent down and greeted her long lost friend, "Hi, Eddie."

"Hi, Marisol," Eddie answered with a smile. "I heard you and your boyfriend finally got Brian some help yesterday. Thank you for that, sweetie."

"He's not my…" Sola started. But then knowing how fleeting her time with Eddie might be, she settled for, "You're welcome."

"Now tell me all about him. Does he have a big dick like the Russian director?" He stage whispered. "He doesn't want to tell me, but I bet he does!"

Which was how Sola came to find herself giggling with Eddie while Ivan made the first of several calls to clean up the body of her dead boyfriend.

Her Russian Brute

Chapter 27

Two Weeks Later

"Are you sure about this, sir?" Gregory asked, his usually calm voice agitated.

They stood together at the solarium's window, watching Hannah walk their guest back to the house. She'd just finished showing him the other outbuildings on the property. It was the exact same tour Hannah had given Ivan when he arrived last spring, but Hannah didn't seem nearly as warm and engaged with the man beside her as she had with him. Perhaps because he was yet another outsider—a large Greek this time, as opposed to a monstrous Russian—but an outsider nonetheless.

In the wide back meadow, a black helicopter—the third to set down in as many weeks—waited patiently for its only passenger to return.

"I'm not sure he'll fit in here," Gregory told Ivan now, the closest the old servant had ever come to directly questioning one of Ivan's decisions.

248

Ivan cut his eyes at the man, getting the same feeling he had this morning when he'd heard Hannah talking to someone in his office.

"He just told us he's selling the property," he'd heard her say as he approached the study. "The buyer's due here any minute… No, I didn't know he was interested in selling. If I had, I would certainly have had him call you first, King Nightwolf…"

Ivan stopped in his tracks as soon as he heard her, careful not to make a sound as he listened in. But the old woman abruptly ended the call. "He's coming, I have to go," she said quickly.

By the time he reached the door, she was back to cleaning his office. The rotary phone now sitting in a new position on his desk, the only sign she'd made a call at all.

And now here was Gregory, questioning his decision to sell Wolfson Manor to another outsider.

"I do not fit in here, either," Ivan pointed out. Perhaps Gregory had forgotten how little welcome this strange mountain town had given him so far. "Also, according to his portfolio, he has several such properties around the world, many located in small mountain towns just like this one. I think he is a collector of sorts, and he

Her Russian Brute

quickly agreed to my term to keep you two on as caretakers for the property. Do not worry, Gregory. I doubt you will see him all that often, and there will be no need for him to—as you say… fit in."

However, his words didn't seem to bring Gregory any solace. "I know you're probably doing this because you're still upset about that wolf attack, and I'm sorry about that. You'll never know how sorry I am…"

Ivan shrugged. "It is not your fault."

"I—that wolf could have hurt Miss Sola or you or done worse. I should have done more to make sure she understood the dangers of going out on full moon nights. But that's no reason to sell the kingdom house. Especially to this fellow. He smells…wrong. Hannah thinks so, too."

Ivan squinted at the thin man, wondering how he could possibly know that, given he and Hannah hadn't had a chance to exchange words since the buyer's arrival. At least not that Ivan had seen.

But this wasn't the first time the couple seemed to know what the other was thinking. Yet another strange thing about Wolfson Point. That, and the townspeople's weird turns of phrase when it came to this manor house and its prior occupant. Also, the strange full moon curfew,

250

accompanied as it was by the sudden soundtrack of howling wolves. He continued to be mystified by the town he'd chosen to hide out in.

But not for much longer.

"It's already done," Ivan told Gregory. "The papers have been signed. This inspection is just a formality."

Gregory gave in with a tired sigh. "Yes, I thought as much when you took Sola away. I suppose you'll be joining her in California now?"

"*Nyet*," Ivan answered, not giving the question even a moment of indulgent thought.

Gregory seemed to be gearing up for another question, but before he could get it out, the buyer entered the solarium with Hannah.

Hannah's face remained neutral, but the fact that her usual warm smile was nowhere in sight spoke volumes about her discomfort with this man, much more than any outward signs of nervousness would have.

Ivan could understand both her and Gregory's unease. He didn't meet very many men larger than he was, but Damianos Drákon—with his mane of thick, black hair—was such a man. He was even bigger than his cousin Boris, with rippling muscles that barely seemed contained by his very expensive dark suit.

Yet, despite his excess of muscle, Damianos was the very picture of refined elegance. He looked fairly young— no more than a decade older than Ivan, if that. Yet he carried himself with even more confidence than any of the gentlemen Ivan had met from some of Russia's oldest and most exclusive families. In fact, he seemed to reek of a sort of old-world civility, which made Ivan question how he'd come into his money.

For this buyer was someone you didn't very often find these days: a discreet billionaire. One Ivan had never heard of before he'd approached Alexei, asking if his younger cousin might be amenable to selling his Idaho property.

"Was everything to your liking?" Ivan asked the mysterious buyer.

"Of course," he answered with a polite bow of his head. "Hannah was very gracious to show me the property. I must take my leave now, but I am well-pleased with this acquisition, and I am most grateful to each of you for taking the time to meet with me."

Ivan held out his hand for the final shake. "You're welcome, Mr. Drákon. Please take care of Hannah and

252

Gregory. They have been good to me, and I hope you will be good to them."

"Of course," the buyer answered, taking Ivan's hand in a firm clasp that reminded him of old movies featuring toga-clad Roman Emperors.

Damianos had a Greek accent, but one tinged with an archaic formality unlike anything Ivan had encountered before. And as they shook, he once more had the unsettling feeling that despite this man's outwardly youthful appearance, he was dealing with someone quite old.

"And now that we have completed our business together, you must call me Anos, as all my friends do."

"Anos," Ivan repeated. "I have enjoyed doing business with you."

Ivan carefully ignored the stricken looks on Hannah and Gregory's faces. Their lives would be easier without having to serve a grumpy Russian, and he could not risk Sola seeking him out here.

The memory of her holding that broken man's hand continued to haunt him, even though they had now officially been apart longer than they'd been together.

You are not the man she deserves, he reminded

Her Russian Brute

himself, just as he'd been reminding himself every day since they parted. He wouldn't be another broken thing for her to take care of.

Ivan had plans. Plans that could not include her, no matter how much his heart ached for the woman who'd turned his world upside down and taught him to finally start looking beyond himself.

As soon as the Greek's helicopter departed, Ivan picked up the rotary phone to arrange for a helicopter of his own. It was time. Finally time to move on.

Chapter 28

It was exactly like what happened with her father all over again. One moment, Ivan was there in her life, making calls, then issuing clipped orders to the small crew of men in generic maintenance clothes who answered the first of those calls.

The men worked quickly. Rolled a large carpet in and then rolled the same carpet with Scott's body inside, out.

A doctor and nurse arrived on the heels of their departure. A man and a woman respectively, both dressed in casual business attire. The doctor looked Eddie over with a small penlight. Meanwhile the nurse took care of reviving poor Vanessa with smelling salts, which Sola didn't even know was a thing anymore.

"Poor Vanessa is having quite the week," Eddie observed from his seat.

Yes, she was. Yet, somehow Ivan managed to smooth that over, too. He and the nurse talked to the little home aide in low, quiet voices, and whatever they said

Her Russian Brute

must have done the trick. Vanessa not only left with the nurse a few minutes later, but Ivan came over to assure them that she would be back after a few weeks of rest and observation. Meanwhile, her cousin would be brought in to cover until she felt up to coming back.

Ivan informed both Sola and Eddie of this, but only one of them was able to answer by the time he came back with the news. Eddie was gone inside himself again, eyes clouded over, the sun of his "good day" gone.

And shortly after Eddie left, Ivan announced his own departure.

Sola walked him to the door. Trying to think of something to say. Desperate to find the right words to convince him to stay.

But he was already gone. She could feel the distance between them, wider than it had ever been, even when he pulled her to him and gave her a long, slow kiss.

Good-bye. It was a kiss good-bye, and it was all Sola could do not to cling to him when he inevitably drew back from her.

"You must stay here with Eddie until the new aide arrives," he told her, cupping the side of her face in his large hand. "I have been assured it will be no more than an

256

hour."

"Thank you," she whispered with tears in her eyes.

"Do not thank me," he answered. One last time. And then he left.

And just like with her father, she couldn't follow him.

* * *

Which was why she ran not walked when a pounding knock sounded on her door a few weeks later. It had to be her Russian, because no one else she knew would knock on a door like that—at least not without yelling "POLICE!" or "INS!" soon after.

But she was wrong. There was a Russian on her doorstep when she swung the door open…but not the one she was expecting. It was Alexei Rustanov and with him stood an older man in a dark suit and…

"Aunt Ximena!" Sola cried, before asking in Spanish, "What are you doing here?"

Her aunt answered in a stream of agitated Spanish about how she didn't understand any of this! Apparently, an INS officer had shown up at the motel where she worked and insisted she come with him. He'd put her on a "very pretty" private plane—something she'd never flown

Her Russian Brute

in before—and brought her all the way down here where this large Russian man had been waiting for them outside the small house, where it turned out Sola lived.

Her aunt looked positively ashen as Alexei escorted her into Sola's house along with the INS officer. And she kept asking both Alexei and the INS suit what was going on, over and over, in broken English.

Only to break down in happy tears ten minutes later when the INS officer instructed both of them to raise their hands to recite the oath of allegiance.

"I apologize for the dramatics, Sola and Ximena," Alexei said somberly after they were both declared naturalized citizens of the United States. "But this had to be done as discreetly as possible. What happened here today is not exactly 'by the book' as Americans—you Americans—might say…"

"We understand," Sola said grinning as she hugged her still sobbing aunt. Ximena was so overcome, she'd barely been able to repeat her parts of the oath. "Thank you, Mr. Rustanov! Thank you so much! You'll never know how much this means to us!"

Alexei shook his head. "Thank Ivan. This was one of the things he insisted on before he left the country."

258

That was when her happiness froze inside her chest.

"What do you mean before he left the country?"

Her Russian Brute

Chapter 29

Six Months Later

He said to tell you he is not the man you deserve.

Like the weirdest fairy godmother ever, Ivan had appeared out of nowhere, improved every aspect of her life for the better within the space of six weeks, only to disappear without a word besides those delivered by his cousin.

Six months later, Alexei's words were still floating around Sola's head. Following her wherever she went. Even as she packed for her second international trip ever, and the first she'd ever taken by plane. If she was still this haunted by the love affair that had been cut unexpectedly short six months ago, she wondered what it would be like when she was actually in St. Petersburg, completing the fellowship Alexei Rustanov had arranged for her.

Sola almost pretended she wasn't home when she heard the knock on her front door. But she couldn't do that. One: it would be mean, and two: her car, a practical

Camry, which had mysteriously appeared along with all of its papers inside the glove compartment just a couple of days after she passed her driver's test, was parked in front of the house. Which meant Brian totally knew she was home.

"Why aren't you dressed yet?" he demanded when she opened the door. Despite finally letting his hair go gray, or perhaps even because of it, Brian had been looking a lot more dapper as of late. But tonight, he looked even more silver fox than usual, dressed in the tux he usually reserved for his opera opening nights.

Sola glanced down at her shorts and t-shirt. Pretty much the official uniform of the California summer. "I thought maybe I'd skip out on tonight," she answered. "I've got so much to do before I leave…"

"No, no," Brian was saying before Sola could even continue rolling out the rest of her excuses. "Put on a black dress right now, young lady! Alexei Rustanov just donated a large sum of money to our program. So when a big donor invites us to his fundraising gala, we go."

"But I'm not even technically a student at ValArts anymore," she pointed out. "And I've only got two more days to pack for two whole years in Russia! He's got to understand that, since he's the one who arranged for me to get the fellowship in the first place..."

"Marisol, you're young, so I'll explain this to you just this once. Big donors do not *understand* when you decide to skip their galas so you can *pack*. That's not how these things work. Now, dearest Marisol, if you'd like to have a successful career directing operas as opposed to assisting those of us who know better than to skip galas thrown by major opera donors, I suggest you get dressed as quickly as possible and put on your make-up in the car."

Well, when he put it that way...

Sola's real reason for not wanting to go to the gala—that anything or anyone with the Rustanov name attached to it reminded her of Ivan and therefore hurt too much—seemed rather pitiful. Especially since she hadn't seen or heard so much as a peep from Ivan in the past six months.

What a jackhole, she thought, not for the first time.

Yes, a jackhole, that was what Ivan was. A jackhole who had saved her life twice, made sure her ex-boyfriend would never hurt her or anyone else ever again, kept the mentor she loved most in the world from destroying himself, ensured that Eddie received 24-hour care, paid for the remainder of her education, and arranged for her to finally get the American citizenship she so desperately needed to make her dreams of directing opera after college come true. Which at the end of the day made it hard for Sola to know how to feel about the Russian who'd change her life for the better, but broke her heart with his decision to utterly vanish.

But that wasn't Brian's fault. And she'd been to enough Friends and Family sessions at New Promises during the ninety days Brian was in Ivan-sponsored rehab to know it probably wasn't a great idea to send him alone to a fundraiser where the champagne would flow.

"Fine," she grumbled. "Give me fifteen minutes."

* * *

"You look beautiful tonight, Sola," Alexei told her a little over an hour later, bringing her hand up for a kiss before introducing her to his pretty Southern wife, Eva.

She was taking Brian's advice and paying court to the king as was his due. Sola stood in the middle of the Institute's ballroom with Alexei and his wife, a glass of barely touched champagne in her hand. Learning to play the game of art was just as important as talent in this business, Brian had told her before nudging her toward the power couple.

Her Russian Brute

Still, she couldn't help but feel intimidated. Eva, who she'd heard about but never met before, was even prettier in person than in all the gushing blog posts she'd read about how the small town mayor and her billionaire husband had turned around their little Texas town. Yet she was the one looking at Sola as if a celebrity had walked into the room.

"So *you're* the girl who got Ivan to come down from his mountain!" Eva said with a huge dazzling smile as she took Sola's hand in both of hers. "Girl, I have been dying to meet you!"

"The pleasure's all mine, Mrs. Rustanov," Sola answered, finding it impossible not to smile back in the face of Eva's almost aggressive enthusiasm.

Then remembering why she'd come over in the first place, she said, "Oh, and thank you, Mr. Rustanov, for the St. Petersburg opportunity. I'm so excited!"

But Alexei only frowned. "What St. Petersburg opportunity?"

"The Alexei Rustanov Opera Fellowship?" she reminded him. "The reason I'll be in Russia for the next two years, interning with the St. Petersburg Opera House?"

264

Alexei shook his head. "I'm sorry, but as talented as I am sure you are, I arranged nothing for you. You must have won that fellowship on your own merit."

But before she could point out that the fellowship literally had his name written all over it, and that she hadn't even applied for it, he said, "Oh, I see our director friend, Mr. Krantz. Eva, come *kotenok*, I would like you to meet him. I need to discuss with him a new piece the Twins have been working on."

They were gone in a flash, leaving Sola with a number of unanswered questions.

As it turned out, quite a few of her program mates had also been invited to the gala, and she was in constant demand as they grabbed her for short conversations about summer plans. But after thirty minutes of watching both Brian and Alexei schmooze at levels she simply wasn't capable of from afar, Sola decided to leave.

It was obvious Brian was having a much easier time than she was at this party. And Alexei and Eva were surrounded by so many other big donors and university officials, she doubted she'd be getting anywhere near them again any time soon.

Meanwhile, Sola was becoming more and more

Her Russian Brute

antsy by the minute. It was as if a weird, dissonant soundtrack was looping in the background of her psyche, ratcheting up her anxiety and making her feel edgy the way she did when she'd had too much caffeine. She felt like something was approaching, but she didn't know what.

"Calling an Uber" she texted Brian. *"See you tomorrow for breakfast."*

Another good thing that had come out of Brian's stint in rehab: they'd begun sharing breakfast every morning like a real family. And more often than not, it was during this time that the old Eddie would come out to talk with them, if only for a few minutes.

Sola left, hoping Brian wouldn't be too upset with her, only to run straight into a wall when she walked through the door.

"Leaving so soon?"

No, it wasn't a wall…

She looked up, and then up some more, to see perhaps one of the most beautiful men she'd ever beheld in her entire life. Another Rustanov maybe? Like Ivan and his hockey player cousin, he had blond hair. He also had Ivan's piercing blue eyes. But aside from that, the two didn't share anything in common.

This man was dressed in a tux, and he looked so comfortable in it, Sola actually found herself wondering if he hadn't perhaps been born in one. Also, unlike Ivan, his hair was slicked back in a stylishly coiffed look that would have easily qualified him to model in one of those *we're way classier than you* designer cologne ads.

Still, there was something about this man… Something that made her breathe out the question in her heart, even though it was an impossibility.

"Ivan?"

Chapter 30

To Ivan, the look on Sola's face was worth it. The painful series of final surgeries. The torturous months of recovery. Every agonizing second he'd gone through was more than worth it just to see her like this.

"*Da*, Sola, it's me," he said, clasping her around the shoulders. "I wondered if you would still recognize me. The doctors had to alter my face somewhat in order to fix it."

"I can't believe it…!" she said, her voice filled with the same shock and wonder clearly etched across her face. "I just can't believe it!"

"Neither can I," Ivan answered her truthfully. "But the doctors Alexei found for me are very skilled."

"Obviously." She reached up and tentatively, oh so softly, touched the previously scarred side of his face. "Is this real?"

"*Da*. It's a combination of my own skin grafted with artificial skin created by a 3-D printer. It's completely safe for you touch with whatever amount of pressure you wish."

"Are you sure?" Sola asked, her tone both scared and doubtful.

"I promise you, Sola, I am completely healed."

"Oh, good! Then I can do this…"

With only that small warning, his little Sola hauled back and slapped him hard across his brand new face.

Ivan's head flinched to the side, more out of surprise than anything else, but then he looked back at her, enjoying the glint in Sola's fierce brown eyes. Oh, how he'd missed that righteous indignation of hers during the past several months. "You still have the ability to surprise me, Sola."

As glad as he was to see her, she looked nothing but furious to see him. Even though he was now one hundred times easier to look at.

"What kind of man—no…what kind of *jackhole,* just ups and vanishes like that? You made me love you, and then you just took off!"

"You love me?" he repeated, his heart filling with wonder despite her other much angrier words.

"You basically made every dream I've ever had come true. Even the ones I didn't know I should have.

Her Russian Brute

Yes, of course I love you! But then you just…disappeared."

He tried to answer, but his beautiful Sola raged on before he could.

"And you didn't even have the balls to tell me you were leaving the country! Instead you had your cousin do your 'Dear John' dirty work! And then six months go by without a word. How could you do that? To me? To us?!?!"

"I am sorry, Sola," he said, cupping her shoulders. "But I knew I wasn't the man you deserved. Not with the face I had before..."

She shook her head, eyes blazing, "I told you…"

"I know what you told me, Sola, and I believe you. But *I* cared. That face belonged to the man I used to be. The killer who only lived for revenge. I wanted—I needed to be better than a man who hides himself away from the world for you. More than the Russkie monster too scared to come out of the manor and live in the light with you. That's why I left. But now I have this new face, and I used the time in recovery to set up that program for promising opera fellows from around the world at the St. Petersburg Opera."

270

Her eyes widened behind her glasses. Black now, with colorful flower details painted across the top and edges. They were unreasonably adorable—just like her. And he found himself missing her that much more, even though he was finally standing right in front of her.

"That was you? But it's named after your cousin, Alexei…"

"Actually, the fellowship is named after my father. He and Alexei shared the same name after a Rustanov ancestor, and I wanted…" He looked away from her for a moment, struggling to come up with the right words. "…I wanted to do something good in my father's name. Finally."

He squeezed her shoulders and continued, "I've also been talking to my cousins. They've helped me through a lot these last few months, and though I used to think I wanted nothing to do with the family business, I have changed my mind. Like you, Alexei and Boris have shown me more kindness than I deserve and now I wish to pay them back with my service. But that means I must finish my university studies…in St. Petersburg."

He moved his hands down her arms to take her hands in his. "So you see, Sola, I've spent these last

Her Russian Brute

months setting up a life for us in Russia. One we could both enjoy together. And now that I've fixed myself, I am presenting myself to you. A better man, the kind of man you deserve."

He had never felt or said anything more sincere in his life, but she looked away from him like his words cut her to the bone.

"The man I deserve...." she repeated with a bitter shake of her head.

And her voice sounded pained when she said, "But you planned all of this without me! You talked to your cousins, arranged for that fellowship—without saying a word to me about *any* of it. Not a call...not an email...not even a text..."

"Sola..." he pleaded. "It was something I had to do on my own. Please understand."

"Meanwhile, I'm out here in California, barely able to keep it together enough to make it through the school year because you just took off after killing my ex-boyfriend!" Sola continued on like he hadn't said anything.

Ivan shifted uncomfortably. "Sola, I missed you every single moment I was away—"

272

"Yeah, well..." Sola yanked her hands back from him. "Now you're really going to miss me!"

Then she surprised him yet again by shoving past him and walking out of his life mere minutes after he'd walked back into hers.

Chapter 31

Sola could only imagine how Ivan felt as he watched her walk away. The complete opposite of whatever he'd been hoping for when he showed up at Alexei's gala with his movie star makeover.

All those surgeries he'd endured, and all the things he'd done to make sure she ended up in St. Petersburg with him. He probably thought she'd just fall into his arms like the last six months had never happened.

But not Sola. Instead, she'd slapped him and stormed off, giving Sirena Rustanov—the best and only opera diva she knew—a run for her dramatic money.

Stormed off so well, Ivan could only watch her leave in stunned silence, as his months of effort and planning turned to ashes.

Stormed off so well, she knew he was completely surprised when he returned to his limo shortly after her dramatic exit to find her leaning up against the car door, with her arms crossed over the plunging neckline of her little black dress.

"Sola?" he said, big head crooking to the side as if he weren't sure she was real, or just a figment of his imagination.

"That back there," she said, jabbing her finger toward the steps where Ivan had made his huge announcement, "is *not* how you do a dramatic reveal."

Then she turned her hand, palm up, and circled it slowly just in front of her face. "*This* is how you do a dramatic reveal."

Ivan stared at her, the very picture of incredulity, for moments on end. But then his lips spread into wide smile.

"Sola," he said, his tone now indulgent. "You never cease to surprise me."

It was finally her turn to grin, to let Ivan off the hook for making her suffer without his big, stupid, best-she-ever-had self.

"Good, now you get it," she told him softly, stringing her arms around his thick neck. "Don't *ever* try to out-surprise an opera nerd. You, sir, need to stay in your lane."

"Hmmm. If I were you, I would not claim victory just yet," Ivan answered.

Then seemingly out of nowhere, an octagon-shaped

leather box appeared in the space between them.

Sola's eyes widened when he flipped it open with one large thumb to reveal a dazzling diamond ring. "Surprise, Sola, I love you, too."

Sola could only cover her mouth with both hands. "Oh, Ivan…" she whispered, her brown eyes filling with happy tears.

"We have 'just this one life to live,'" he reminded her, quoting Sola's own words back at her. "And I want to live the rest of mine with you."

Less than five minutes later, and one word uttered by Ivan—a word Sola could only assume meant "scram" in Russian—they were once again in the back of a limo.

But unlike the last time, their passion was dialed up several notches, thanks to the ring now gracing Sola's left hand. And the promises they'd made to be together forever.

It was their first time seeing each other in six months and neither was interested in playing it cool. Sola immediately swung a leg over his big body, climbing on top of him with a desperation she couldn't disguise. Ivan had his pants unzipped and his hands beneath the narrow skirt of Sola's black cocktail dress, by the time she got into position on top of him.

They both groaned when he pushed her panties aside, and sank her down onto his naked cock. Both his large hands fisted in her hair, and he pulled her to him for a long, hungry kiss. For minutes on end, all either of them knew was the feel of each other. Lips crashing, bodies rolling together as the smell of their combined sex filled up the limo's back seat.

"Don't stop!" Sola cried, even though he had no intention of doing so.

"I won't," he promised, voice little more than a guttural whisper. "You saved me from myself. You loved me at my ugliest. I will never stop. Not until we are both dead."

That was it. Sola came undone, the orgasm cresting over her in the aftermath of his promise. And he came soon after, still crooning in her ear about what their future would look like together. How it would be for them as husband and wife. How he'd spend the rest of his life proving to her that he'd finally become the man she deserved.

Her Russian Brute

Epilogue

Two Years Later

Life was totally fair. In fact, as far as Sola was concerned, the scales were now over tipped in her favor. She had a wonderful husband who would soon be taking over as president of the Rustanov's Moscow headquarters. And at the very young age of twenty-six, she was set to direct her first opera at the Moscow National Opera. It was a production of one of her favorite new works, *Chrysanthemum,* financed by Alexei and starring her hugely talented in-law, Sirena Rustanov, reprising the titular lead role she'd first debuted in New Mexico.

No, there was no doubt about it. Sola was blessed. Just unbelievably blessed and—

"Give me that note again!" Sirena called up to her from the stage, her down-home Virginia accent ringing out angry and clear across the theater space. "See what happens!"

Behind her, the stage techs and actors were

scrambling to get the props, scenery, and people in place for another run through of the opera's final scene. But while they were rushing to do Sola's bidding, Sirena was downstage rolling her neck at her young director.

"See what happens if you give me that note again! See. What. Happens. Cuz I don't know if you remember this, since you were only, what…like, *three* back then? But I *originated* this role, little girl. You do *not* get to tell me how to sing this character!"

"I truly do not know why she keeps giving Sirena this note," Boris stage-whispered in English to his brother Alexei so Sola couldn't help but hear. The two men were seated just behind her. "Could you talk to her, *Lyosha*?"

Funny how Boris, the man who'd taught her husband to kill, the man who stood north of six-foot-seven and didn't look like anyone's little anything, became a total younger brother with his big brother, the opera financer, whenever the subject involved his opera diva wife. Emphasis on *diva*.

"I have talked to her," Alexei answered in English in the same loud stage-whisper. "She tells me 'I am director and you are not.' She makes Ivan happy, but not so much me."

Her Russian Brute

"Or me," Boris agreed, in his darkest tone.

"I love my in-laws," Sola chanted to herself over and over again: *"I love my in-laws! Love. Them..."*

After all, she reminded herself, they were the ones helping to make her long held dreams come true. Why, in less than a week, Brian—who'd somehow managed not to relapse into alcoholism after Eddie's sad but inevitable death just over a year ago—would be sitting here in this very seat. She was *blessed* and life was *fair*. So fair. *So, so fair...*

"You look like you're reminding yourself how fair your life is again" Ivan whispered, dropping down in the seat next to hers. As per usual, he was dressed in a suit. Today's selection was light blue, which went perfectly with his blond hair and brought out his eyes. It was all too easy to see how he'd recently made it onto a popular American women's magazine's list of the world's 50 sexiest businessmen, even though he'd only technically been a C-level at Rustanov Moscow for two months.

"Yes, that's exactly what I'm doing..." she groaned, leaning over to kiss him.

"What now?"

"I've only got two more days of dress rehearsal, and

Sirena's refusing to take my advice about not holding the last note of the last aria so long. Meanwhile, your cousins are behind me throwing shade like this is *The Muppet Show*.

Ivan's eyes narrowed. "I know shade, but not *The Muppet Show*."

"Remember the green frog and his pig girlfriend? Oh never mind, I'll show you some YouTube clips tonight. Anyway, there are these two old men puppets who sit in a theater and criticize everything and everyone in the show. And they're *almost* as annoying as your two cousins."

Ivan glanced over his shoulder at the two older men, who in the way of shit-starters the world over, waved back at him like everything was fine.

I still owe my cousins a lot for the putting up with me in spite of the terrible things I said and did before you made me want to be a better man." He shifted in his seat to level with her, voice low and confidential: "But for you, I will go back to old ways. For you, I can make sure they never bother you again."

"Aw…" She smiled at him, patting his cheek with affection. "Thank you for offering to take out your cousins for me, babe. That's very Rustanov of you. But it's okay,

Her Russian Brute

I've got this…"

She stood suddenly and yelled out, "Sirena, either break the note off before the one minute mark, or be okay with the curtain closing on you if you don't."

Then before the diva could respond, she announced, "And if *anyone* other than me wants to keep talking during *my* rehearsal, let me know so I can call security to escort you out."

She could feel Alexei and Boris's petulant glares burning into her back, but she didn't hear another word from them after she sat back down.

"This is why I love you, Sola," Ivan said, grinning at her when she was back in her seat. "You are so little, but so fierce. And you are still the most surprising."

"I love you, too," she said, grinning back at him. "But speaking of surprises, why are you here?"

Ivan sobered then, and a shadow crossed his face. "The woman who served as maid of honor at our wedding…the one you flew back to see when she graduated from medical school—Anitra, yes? Anitra Dunhill?"

"Dr. Anitra Dunhill," Sola corrected, knowing just how hard her best friend had worked to earn that title.

Ivan only frowned. "I was afraid of that."

He took out his phone and showed her a post with a screaming headline.

Sola's eyes widened. "No, that's impossible! She would not have gotten married. Not without telling me. And definitely not to someone like him!"

But before Ivan, who didn't know Anitra nearly as well as Sola did, could answer, she was grabbing her own phone and placing an international call to her best friend's West Virginia number. Only to curse when it went straight to voicemail.

"Is this article I'm reading true?" Sola demanded as soon as her friend's easygoing voice promised to get back to her. "And if so, what the hell, Anitra! Why would you marry—actually *marry*—somebody like that?!?! Call me back as soon as you get this!"

* * *

Whoa! Whoa! Whoa! Why is Sola so upset? Who did Anitra marry?!?!
Find out in Theodora Taylor's next release, HIS FORBIDDEN BRIDE!

* * *

Her Russian Brute

Oh, my gosh!!!

I can't believe this series is finally finished. I've had so much fun with the Rustanov family and their quirky loves, that I can hardly believe their story is done. Well, at least their story is done for now. I've learned you never know who will show up next in one of my books, and there's at least one Rustanov offspring who will make an appearance in my upcoming, next-generation Viking Shifters Saga!

Speaking of which, what was up with that strange little Idaho mountain town? This won't be the last time my contemporary and shifter universes collide, so make sure you're all caught up by checking out my bestselling time-travelling shifter series!

That said, I am beyond thrilled you joined me for this series. What a wild, hot, and sweet ride! If you enjoyed Ivan and Sola's story, please show your love by leaving a review on Amazon.

So much love!
Theodora Taylor

About the Author

Theodora Taylor writes hot books with heart. When not reading, writing, or reviewing, she enjoys spending time with her amazing family, going on date nights with her wonderful husband, and attending parties thrown by others. She now lives in Los Angles, California, and she LOVES to hear from readers. So drop her a line or friend her on Facebook. And, if you love Interracial Romance as much as she does, sign up for her IR Weekly Bestsellers newsletter!

Also by Theodora Taylor

HOT CONTEMPORARIES WITH HEART

The Owner of His Heart

The Wild One

Her Perfect Gift

His One and Only

His for Keeps

His for the Summer

His Pretend Baby

HOT RUSSIANS WITH HEART

Her Russian Billionaire

Her Russian Surrender

Her Russian Beast

Her Russian Brute

HOT HARLEQUINS WITH HEART

Vegas Baby

Love's Gamble

HOT PARANORMALS WITH HEART

Her Viking Wolf

Wolf and Punishment

(The Alaska Princesses Trilogy, Book 1)

Wolf and Prejudice

(The Alaska Princesses Trilogy, Book 2)

Wolf and Soul

(The Alaska Princesses Trilogy, Book 3)

Her Viking Wolves

HOT SUPERNATURAL WITH HEART

His Everlasting Love

CPSIA information can be obtained
at www.ICGtesting.com
Printed in the USA
FFOW02n2054020118
44327174-43968FF